J. D. Clockman

THE UNIVERSITY OF ODIUM

London
Jetstone
2015

A *Jet*stone paperback original.

ISBN 9781910858011

Cover design by The Ever-Shifting Subject.

Contents

PART ONE
20 SEPTEMBER

Chapter One

20 September

Two men stood facing each other in post-handshake awkwardness.

The one who had introduced himself as the Registrar said with professional breeziness, "You have me at a disadvantage, Professor. I've just moved back into this office after summer redecoration and it's taking me a while to unpack things." He gestured with a handsweep to the cheap wooden crates littering the expensively wooded room.

The other man, who was in his early sixties, seemed to know that the Registrar, who was in his late fifties, was wondering how his secretaries had been bypassed. This other had introduced himself as the Professor when the first man had introduced himself as the Registrar. Now he said, "Buckrack."

The word sounded, to the Registrar, like some kind of insult.

"I beg your pardon?" said the Registrar.

"Professor Buckrack," said Professor Buckrack.

"Oh!" the Registrar chortled. "Of course. I am Dr Asterisk. But I prefer it if senior members of the academic staff call me Nigel. Some of them insist on calling me the

Registrar, which seems a little over-formal."

Buckrack allowed nothing to be said for an interval. Once the interval had become uncomfortable for Asterisk, he replied, still standing, and with a look at the boxes on the floor, "So, Asterisk, you mean it's taking a while for you to get someone to unpack the stuff for you?"

Furrows appeared on Asterisk's disconcerted brow.

Buckrack continued, "I went into your main office before I came in here, the large open plan one next door, where all your support staff work. Their packing cases were all being removed. They finished emptying them yesterday. Of course, they unpacked themselves."

In an English accent, suffused with some vague historical right to moralism, these observations might have been taken as an affront. In Buckrack's broad Californian, infused with an edgy Bogartian menace, they prompted guardedness rather than retaliation. Asterisk smiled. The excessiveness of the smile gave the appearance of unctuousness, behind which the reality was possibly little different. So Buckrack mused while Asterisk stepped over the crack in the conversation.

"I simply meant I did not have the relevant paperwork concerning you to hand," he explained. "Of course the Vice Chancellor did mention to me that you would be arriving, I knew that. Usually, though, you would see him rather than me. That's why you find me a little unprepared."

Buckrack grunted. "Yeah, Covet's not in town," he said routinely.

Asterisk evenly replied, "Sir Evan... The Vice Chancellor, yes, that's right."

"Where is he?" asked Buckrack sharply.

Asterisk looked puzzled. "I'm unsure, to be honest. It doesn't seem to matter much these days. International calls are so cheap, one is always connected, one's Blackberry is always on, there is little reason to ask."

Before Asterisk had concluded Buckrack had taken out an iPhone and speed dialled. It was at his ear by the time Asterisk had finished. "Or to tell," Buckrack said, as the number he had called started to ring. Asterisk watched, fascinated by the man's astringency with words, and what seemed his unprofessorial directness.

"Hey, Covet," Buckrack hollered into the phone. "Where are you?"

At this Asterisk's eyes widened.

"What's happening, you ask?" Buckrack waxed on, turning his back on Asterisk, stepping fluidly across the crate-strewn floor, and taking a seat on an ornamental *chaise longue*, from which vantage point he stared out of the window across the quadrangle, his face three quarters hidden from Asterisk.

Asterisk hissed with concern, "I think he's in the States!" and was ignored. "It's the middle of the night there!" Still he got no reaction.

"Singapore, huh?" Buckrack turned briefly and looked sideways at Asterisk. "There's a place called The Swastika Hotel not far from the airport. Never been in it, but when I see it *en route* I always think of you, you being so Buddhistic and all."

Asterisk, upon whom a feeling was dawning that he had entered the ring as a boxer only to discover that he was actually the referee, noted that this was said without the obvious traces of humour that might allow one to detect that it was mere joshing. The Vice Chancellor was a Presbyterian and did not much indulge in irony of the kind that must have been intended in Buckrack's last remark. Asterisk continued to listen, with increasing curiosity and decreasing self-confidence.

"Yeah, never mind. Listen, Covet, your man Asterix here, he seems not to have been briefed. You won't mind filling him in."

To Asterisk's consternation, Buckrack proffered the phone with his left hand over his left shoulder, all the while continuing to look away, his face turned to the window. Asterisk crossed the room gingerly and took the phone. Buckrack stayed where he was. Asterisk retreated to his previous position and, perplexed by the body language of Buckrack, turned half away and supported himself lightly on his buttocks on the edge of his substantial escritoire, which occupied the area of a ping pong table, but was ten times the mass and fifty times the density. He cleared his throat.

"Vice Chancellor," he warmed. "My apologies, I thought you might be at the meeting in Chicago."

A second later, Asterisk hauled himself off the desk, almost to attention. "Yes, Vice Chancellor!" he affirmed. Then he smelled something acrid. He turned his head and, to his astonishment, saw that Buckrack had lit a cigarette. The American continued to face the quadrangle, his demeanour unreadable.

The trebly squeak of a raised voice in the earpiece of the phone reached even Buckrack's ears, although he could not make out the individual words. Asterisk stood even more erect, yet the stiffened stance had the curious effect, Buckrack saw, as he watched the reflection in the window pane, of making him appear more, not less, discomposed.

"Of course, Vice Chancellor," repeated Asterisk, but with no joviality this time. "Go ahead. Do you mind if I make notes?"

There was another harsh squawk from the phone.

"I see, nothing in writing. Understood. Do go on, Vice

Chancellor."

Buckrack counted sixteen *sotto voce* expressions in the side of the conversation on which he then eavesdropped. There were two *indeed*s, four *of course*s, one *naturally*, a further *understood*, a pair of *I see*s, a *really*, two *I shall*s, one *without fail*, one *I'll take care of it*, and one final *golly*. The first non-phatic thing Asterisk said was some time after Buckrack had dropped his cigarette into the dregs of a convenient coffee cup he had been using as an ashtray. The utterance signalled the end of the monologue from Asterisk's interlocutor, and seemed a gloss on what Asterisk had heard. It was said in a titter that implied a humorous attempt to show understanding and complicity with shady matter: "A covert ops kind of thing, then."

This provoked a high pitched, unmistakably berating rasp from the phone which was, like the others, indecipherable.

"Oh no, Vice Chancellor, I'm not taking it *too* seriously," Asterisk reassured. "But I know that I should take it *somewhat* seriously."

This was said as if to demonstrate that a profound nostrum had been learned and was now engrained. Then, as if to fill up a silence, Asterisk went on, "Vice Chancellor, you know that I shall – ". But there he stopped and fumbled for a button. The silence evidently meant that the call had been unritualistically terminated on the other end.

There was a longish pause. Buckrack did not stir. Asterisk moved the phone in his hand pensively a few times. He was breathing deeply. He was striving for grace under pressure, a pose he liked, and a phrase he used a good deal. The effort made him forget Buckrack for a moment. He put the phone on the desk.

"That's not yours," said Buckrack almost instantly, still facing the window. At last he turned. It seemed an invitation to Asterisk to take a seat beside him on his own *chaise*. Asterisk slowly acquiesced, but had to stop halfway across the room and turn around to retrieve the phone, which he then held out to Buckrack. The American took the phone, examined it, and pressed a button on it.

"I am sorry, I thought I had hung up," said Asterisk, sitting down and leaning too far back. He propped himself correctively forward.

"You did," Buckrack replied.

Asterisk took another deep breath, which helped him rally.

"Well," he said. "Professor Buckrack."

Buckrack said nothing.

Asterisk waved his arm in the air gallantly. "Everything seems to be in order," he said. "The paperwork is all taken care of, I understand, and I am told you don't need the customary tour, or the usual round of introductions. The Vice Chancellor looks forward to seeing you when he returns, and you report directly to him."

"That's right," said Buckrack. "It was you who needed to be briefed, not me. But I might need to talk to you again, given that Covet won't be back for a while."

"Oh." Asterisk bobbed slightly on the seat. "You know when he's returning?"

"Yes," said Buckrack. But he did not enlighten Asterisk as to when.

Asterisk smiled apologetically. "Yes." He pressed his hands together. "I must apologise. I was unaware."

Buckrack put his phone in the top pocket of his jacket. "Of what?" he said.

"Of the terms of your appointment. I thought you were the usual kind of Professor."

"I see."

A pause lengthened into another silence with which Buckrack seemed at ease but in which Asterisk appeared agitated.

"Universities these days are places where one should not simply assume things," he said. "I should have asked before the Vice Chancellor left. I made the mistake of assuming."

Buckrack still said nothing.

Asterisk added, "But everything's cleared up now."

Buckrack arose. Asterisk stayed where he was. Looking up, eyes necessarily widened, with a little bit of visionary inspiration suddenly appearing in them, he said warmly, "Actually, it's one of the challenging things about the job today. Everything used to be predictable and, I'll be honest, a little dull. But nowadays something unexpected – something you'd never imagine in a traditional English university – happens quite frequently."

"You betcha," said Buckrack, looking at the door.

"But then everything has changed so much," Asterisk continued. "Did you know, for example, that we now have a campus in China and another in India?"

Buckrack did not reply but gazed at Asterisk unblinkingly.

Asterisk gathered himself and stood. "Before you go, if you wouldn't mind, could I ask you something?"

"Go ahead."

Asterisk looked a little embarrassed, but the embarrassment seemed to hold the promise of an enquiry he hoped would be annealing, soothing, more conciliatory than the discourse had felt so far.

"Have you seen *The West Wing*?" he asked.

Buckrack paused impatiently. "Isn't that exactly where we are? I think I even saw a sign."

"Oh," said Asterisk, "of course, this *is* the west wing of this particular building. But I was referring to the American TV series. You know, Martin Sheen, President Bartlet, all that. Do you know it?"

"Sort of," Buckrack said, and decided to reach for another cigarette.

"The Vice Chancellor gave everyone on our Management Board a box set of all seven series, so we're all entirely fanatical about it."

"Let me guess," said Buckrack. "Covet thinks there's a lot you all can learn about running a university from watching a bunch of actors pretend to run the White House?"

Asterisk smiled affirmatively. "And he's right, you know! He's right. The situations are so similar. The dilemmas. The human drama. The characters! And that's what I was wondering. After I finished speaking to the Vice Chancellor, I was wondering which character you were."

Buckrack's eyes narrowed. "Which character am I? Which *West Wing* wannabe am *I*? Well, tell me – it might help me decide – which character are *you*?"

"Well," Asterisk essayed, with a look in his eyes suggestive of attempted but failed modesty, "as the Vice Chancellor is evidently the President..."

"Evidently," agreed Buckrack.

"And he is a lawyer, so..."

"Evidentially," agreed Buckrack.

"Well, I must be Leo McGarry."

"*Really?*" Buckrack whistled softly. "The White House Chief of Staff, huh? Well, who would have guessed? Is that who you are?"

Asterisk nodded enthusiastically. "I think so."

"Well, tell you what," Buckrack smiled, "we'll have a drink some time and talk more about it. But tell me before I go, have you ever seen *24*?"

Asterisk bit his lip slightly and put his head to one side. "I have heard of it. But I can't say I've ever watched an episode."

Buckrack flipped a cigarette between his lips. "Then you don't know who I am." And with that he left the Registrar's study, a cloud of silver tobacco smoke and yellow nicotine dust mushrooming up towards the high ceiling as the pure oak door swung heavily shut.

"Ladies," was Buckrack's terse valediction as he exited through the adjoining secretaries' office. Alison Stilt and Rachel Brace stared at him in the wonderment that comes from realising *no, one hasn't, after all, seen everything*, and then at each other in the same mode through the trailing grey exhaust he left behind, and then yet again with the same sense of novelty in mind at the closed door of Dr Asterisk's chamber. But the door did not remain, as it often did, inscrutably closed. Instead, Asterisk appeared, looking heavy browed and menacing, in the mode of a boy who has been bullied and wishes to revisit the punishment on someone weaker.

"Rachel," he said, levelly, "please come into my office."

Buckrack carried the quarter-smoked cigarette in his hand along the empty ground floor corridor until he exited by swing doors into the quadrangle, where he threw it in the nearest flower tub: salvias, he reckoned, if their height was anything to go by. He removed a small bottle of Listerine from his left coat pocket and swigged from it, washing his mouth out so thoroughly that the trilling echoes of the vigorous gargling could be heard ricocheting from the walls of the small flagstoned yard. It was not exactly, he reflected as he swilled, an Oxford or Cambridge cloister. In flat white limestone, with hardly a hint of ornateness in the masonry, and an angular, unimposing gilded clock tower, the building which enclosed it seemed, if anything, a somewhat shrunken, cake-top rendering of London's Senate House, which was the inspiration, he seemed to remember, for one of the Ministries, though he could not recall which, in Orwell's *Nineteen Eighty-Four*.

A jet of corrupted mouthwash landed in the flower tub and made the still live cigarette go *phut* and expire. Buckrack took out his iPhone and started up the voice recorder app. As he listened cursorily to the preliminary exchange between himself and Covet he marvelled, not for the first time, that the effects of mobile Listerine were almost as convenient as those of the mobile phone. His tonsils and tongue tingled anew with the chemical tang. The disgustingness of the tobacco was almost instantly obliterated. Menthol floated lightly past his adenoidal cavity into the nose, and he was reminded how, for all that England's culture was pathetic and its citizenry pitiable, even in its unimpressive pockets one could find air of clarity and sweetness that seemed undiscoverable on his side of the pond. And it was true enough. The early autumn ventilation up here on University Hill was a hundred times fresher than in LA. Odium might be a crappy little provincial town, but there were still some things here, like that slant of jaundiced morning light tilting through the archway on the left, falling cold and weak and beautiful on the white paving, you could only dream of in California. He allowed this reverie to captivate him for the few seconds until he heard the exchange between Covet and Asterisk commence:

ASTERISK: Vice Chancellor, my apologies, I thought you might be at the meeting in Chicago.

COVET: Oh shut up, Nigel. I'm in bloody Singapore. Stop thinking and pay attention.

ASTERISK: Yes, Vice Chancellor!

COVET: Listen very carefully, Nigel. I don't want any screw ups.

ASTERISK: Of course, Vice Chancellor. Go ahead. Do you mind if I make notes?

COVET: Of course I bloody well mind. You know the drill, Nigel.

ASTERISK: I see, nothing in writing. Understood. Do go on, Vice Chancellor.

COVET: Buckrack has appeared on the scene.

ASTERISK: Indeed.

COVET: He should give every sign of being a grade A bastard.

ASTERISK: Indeed.

COVET: That's because he *is* a grade A bastard. Bastard *summa cum laude*. There's very little else you need to know.

ASTERISK: Of course.

COVET: He has a one-year research contract, and no affiliation to any particular School or Department. There's a reason for that.

ASTERISK: Of course.

COVET: It means he's not accountable to any of the usual peasant mob of Deans, Pro-Vice Chancellors or Professors. In fact, they don't even know about him.

ASTERISK: Of course.

COVET: He has no office, so no one can locate him. He has no University email address, so he leaves no written traces anyone can request under DPA or

FOI. He answers only to me.

ASTERISK: Of course.

COVET: Don't pry. Don't get yourself in any way between him and me unless I deliberately put you there.

ASTERISK: Naturally.

COVET: Otherwise you'll only get crushed.

ASTERISK: Understood.

COVET: Give him whatever he asks for.

ASTERISK: I see.

COVET: You can check with me first if you are uncertain about the, er, legality.

ASTERISK: I see.

COVET: He might make some unusual requests.

ASTERISK: Really?

COVET: Don't query them. Just meet them.

ASTERISK: I shall.

COVET: If they seem wildly beyond reason or budget you just tell him you need my authorisation and call me immediately.

ASTERISK: I shall.

COVET: Nigel, I need you to follow these simple instructions *to the letter*.

ASTERISK: Without fail.

COVET: The man is going to sort out a lot of our problems. We'd better give him a codename. Let's call him *Avenger*. It's best you ingratiate yourself with him. Ensure he's comfortable in his house. Check with Butcher in Estates.

ASTERISK: I'll take care of it.

COVET: The reason I am telling you to keep your nose out of things is that he has special, shall we say, talents. But he's also, er, *dangerous*. Gelignite in the wrong hands.

ASTERISK: Golly.

COVET: That's why everything must be under the usual radar.

ASTERISK: A covert ops kind of thing, then.

COVET: Oh for Christ's sake, Nigel, shut up! Sometimes I think you take my odd White House analogy too seriously.

ASTERISK: Oh no, Vice Chancellor, I'm not taking it *too* seriously. But I know that I should take it *somewhat* seriously. [*Pause*] Vice Chancellor [*Covet hangs up*], you know that I shall –

Buckrack put the phone away, tucked his hands into the pockets of his coat, took in a gulp of cool late September air, and stepped out into the quadrangle. He decided to go for a morning walk.

Chapter Two

20 September

At around the same time as Buckrack was shaking hands with Asterisk, had a TV or movie camera been panning across the front bay window of a house in Baltimore Street in Bigton – a small satellite town about a mile from the west entrance of the University of Odium – it would have shown us a middle-aged man sitting in an armchair beside a zimmer frame in a dressing gown and exhibiting all the other relevant cinematic or televisual signs of terminal illness. As the camera moved it would reveal to us two other people: the back of a young woman in recognisably nurse-like garb retreating into the kitchen beyond the living room, having put two mugs of tea on a table in front of the evidently dying man; and the profile of another man, preparing to consume the second cup, whose age was between that of the nurse and the soon-to-be-corpse. We would gather enough, knowing viewers that we are, of the general situation without any audio, for it would be skilfully done, with years of *mise-en-scène* know-how and more-than-a-BBC budget behind it. There would of course (ah, verisimilitude!) be something to hear anyway: birds twittering, cars in the street, that kind of thing. But for the details of the particular narrative circumstances spoken language would have to kick in. That would not be a problem, because if there were a camera outside the house there would also be conveniently hidden microphones in the room, which would miraculously allow us to hear what was being said for a few seconds even before the camera point of view switched seamlessly to the interior of the comfortable, spacious lounge where we could, without the apparent knowledge of either Cartwright Miller or James Redman, eavesdrop on their hi-fidelity, hi-definition, Dolby 5.1 surround sound conversation (in which the birds and the cars would now sound from behind our heads while their voices would manifest themselves from a position before us).

Miller seemed to be in very good cheer for a man who will be mouldering in the grave by the fifth chapter of this tale. The conversation was clearly just getting going.

"You know," Miller was saying, "I had a call from an academic acquaintance the other day who actually thought that Macmillan nurses were something one in three British people should be grateful to *Harold* Macmillan for? I had to put him right and tell him, no, that old dipshit and his heirs simply made a profit out of publishing your books, my friend. What next, I asked him, eh? Did he think we were going to have Thatcher Alzheimer Clinics? A blasted Heath Healthcare Foundation? How far might his delusions of ex-Conservative Prime Ministerial charity stretch?"

Redman smiled, but seemed cautious about levity combined with cancer. "You seem, well..."

"Well?" retorted Miller. "I'm not at all well. But I am euphoric at the outcome! I've waited three months for this. It's been agonising! So you can imagine."

"Yes, I meant, well, you seem in good spirits, yes."

"It's probably the morphine," Miller rejoined. "Kylie there helped me shoot up ten minutes before you arrived. You know, it's actually quite fun, being a junkie, knowing there are no consequences. No problem chasing the dragon when there is an atom bomb heading straight towards your head, is there?"

Redman inclined his own as yet untargeted head non-committally.

"I'm sorry," said Miller. "I am making you uneasy. Gallows humour is not so funny if you're a healthy sympathetic onlooker. Look, old chap, you've done a fine job on my behalf. Please tell me all about it."

"About my meeting with Asterisk?"

"Yes, and spare me no detail."

Redman addressed his teacup and then sat back, occasionally referring to a file folder on his lap. "Okay. I called him, as I told you when we spoke on the phone briefly last night, around 4pm. He was not keen to have a meeting with me personally. Said he would rather wait until the hearing this morning. Eventually he caved in and offered me an audience at 5.15. I did see Rachel Brace on the way in and there was a meaningful exchange of looks between us, but nothing more. Asterisk was haughty and gave the impression of bearing my presence as some immense favour. There was a little small talk about the Performance Review and pay negotiations while Rachel brought in coffee and said she was leaving. Then he told me he was surprised that I thought there was anything to discuss about what seemed to him a straightforward case, and he asked me to come to the point.

"I enjoyed a few preliminary remarks, made it clear that I was speaking to him with your full knowledge and that I had your permission to speak on your behalf as your Union representative, given that you were medically incapacitated. He did ask how you were, but I don't think he really listened to the answer, though his head made the appropriate movements and his eyes were fitly downcast for a second or two. I then summarised the case a little, recapping how the meeting scheduled for this morning essentially concerned your grievance to the effect that you were prevented from assuming the Directorship of Information Services, a post to which you had been fairly appointed, for which you had been offered a draft contract as yet unsigned by either party, and which you were due to commence at the beginning of August. I told him we considered that there was no defensible reason for their decision not to appoint you but they had so acted because they had discovered that you were terminally ill. I said that the case would be made from your side that they were not prepared to countenance paying you at the Director's rate through an illness of indeterminate length from which you would not return to service, and that instead they decided to leave you, illegally, as Deputy Director. I made the point that this was detrimental to your likely death-in-service benefits or, if you survived, your pension entitlement upon ill-health retirement."

"And how was he through all of that?" asked Miller.

"He seemed bored. He said that he knew all this from the paperwork but that he could absolutely assure me that the grievance was groundless because the assumption on which it rested was false. He indulged in a long windy circumlocution about how valued a colleague you were and how, even had they discovered that you were terminally ill, they would never have dreamed of altering the terms of appointment for the alleged reason. The plain fact of the matter was that they had not known of your condition when they made the decision and that this could be satisfactorily demonstrated. They had simply decided, in the light of recent administrative and funding develop-ments, which he was of course not at liberty to divulge, that there had to be an unexpected restructuring of the management system in Information Services and that your appointment had of necessity to be reconsidered pending the result of that restructuring. They had expected, he claimed, to appoint you to the corresponding post in the new structure, although he could not vouchsafe a date when that might be agreed upon. He regretted that it had come to a grievance hearing. He felt positively sad that you trust the University so little that you can suspect that it would even contemplate such a dirty trick, never mind go through with it, for the reasons alleged. He urged me to ask you to reconsider a course of action he thought you had taken in a state of clouded judgment."

"Did he seem convincing?"

"With what I had in my hand he could hardly have sounded convincing to me. But I think he was convincing to himself. I asked him to confirm that the decision to rescind the offer of contractual employment was taken at the Management Board of 21 July. I then referred to the University's response to your grievance, which carried his signature, and which stated that the institution had no knowledge of your illness until a communication from you of 23 July. He corroborated both dates. At that point I looked him straight in the eye and asked him to reconsider the claim that he knew nothing about it before 23 July. He smiled back at me and said he had no doubt whatsoever. How could he know before you divulged the fact? He opened his palms in a gesture of accused innocence. I thanked him and fell silent."

"How good a liar is he?"

"He's an excellent liar. Not a blush, not a facial tic, full eye contact, sincerity personified."

Miller smiled. "I love it. So, after the silence?"

"The silence lasted a good five seconds. It seemed to puzzle him. He started to look at me as if I were a little unbalanced. He said, 'Is that it? You asked to meet me just to check facts which, as I have said, are already stated in the papers?' I said no, that I had come to show him a piece of paper we had withheld so far because of its sensitivity. And then I put it on his desk in front of him. He picked it up with exasperated patience and began to read it with histrionic tolerance. It would be about three lines in that I swear I saw the hairs begin to stand up on his head, as he realised what he was looking at."

Miller was almost biting his nails. "Christ, I wish I could have been there!" he hissed.

"I admit it was enjoyable," said Redman. "I said to him, 'Dr Asterisk, that is a word-accurate transcript of part of a telephone conversation you had with the Vice Chancellor about Mr Miller on 19 July. I draw particular attention to your words, *the doc says the sad loser is on his way out,* and the Vice Chancellor's reply, *then put the brakes on the dying fucker.* The entire exchange makes it clear that you both had explicit knowledge of Mr Miller's condition from a named source in the Medical School, and that you were deciding to withdraw the offer of promotion to Director from him on those exact grounds.'"

"Said the spider to the fly!" rejoiced Miller, and then coughed phlegmily, and waved at Redman to go on.

"Of course he looked horrified, but was trying to keep this from seeming too obvious. If his head and brain had been made of glass I am sure I would have seen a lightning storm of electrical impulses flashing from synapse to synapse. But all he could think to say, in a tone of insincere moral outrage, was: 'This is *monstrous*! Where did you get this?'

"I said, 'The recording is now in the Union's possession. It was made by you yourself on your own mobile phone.'

"He threw the paper on the desk. 'Rubbish!' he said. 'Even if that were true, how could you possibly know that or obtain it? This is a fabrication. Why would I do that?'

"I replied, 'I can only guess, but knowing this University as I do, I imagine it's one of a number of illegal and/or immoral acts the Vice Chancellor has asked you to commit and that you were recording the conversation surreptitiously as a kind of insurance for yourself in the event of being found out. It would prove that you were simply acting on his orders. Unwittingly, that's exactly what the recording does allow us, the Union, to prove, as well as demonstrating that a University Hospital consultant breached doctor-patient confidentiality to you personally. Your signature on the response to the grievance proves that you lied about the date on which you learned of Mr Miller's illness.'

"He was goggle-eyed by now. 'But it's useless. You cannot use illegally obtained voice recordings in a court or an employment tribunal!'

"I told him that only he and the Vice Chancellor and the doctor had done anything illegal, or immoral, or unprofessional, or all three. The recording was legally obtained and the Union was not intending to use it in a legal setting.

"'How did you get it?' he asked.

"I told him straight: 'It was copied from the memory card in your phone.'

"By this point he was bewildered. 'You stole my

phone?'

"I said, 'No one stole your phone.'

"More bemusement. 'But how?'

"I said, 'You will have to work that out for yourself, Dr Asterisk. I assure you no one stole your phone or hacked into it or did anything illegal in respect of it. I acknowledge that there was arguably a breach of privacy but then, as the phone is actually University property, and the content of the call records illegal intent, I don't think anyone is going to think there was not good reason for that. And I very much doubt if it needs an employment tribunal to make the evidence effective. We were thinking more of what would happen if its contents were revealed by the media. You will consider the consequences of that – for you, for the Vice Chancellor, for the member of staff in the Medical School, for the University's public reputation.'

"I suppose by this time his subjective state was rather like someone who has been in a car crash and comes round finding himself trapped in his seat with flames and smoke visible in the rear-view mirror. There was a long, shocked pause. And then he said – "

"No!" Miller interrupted. "Let me guess. He flung his arms out and said, 'What do you want from me?' That's what they all do on the TV."

Redman smiled. "No. He put his head in his hands and said, 'Oh, crap!', which was a much better line. Then he did pretty much ask what I was after. So I told him that we wanted to prevent the grievance hearing from taking place today, or else I would have no choice but to table the evidence at that meeting. The easiest solution to the entire matter would be to honour the original decision to promote you so that you were in post, with the Director's salary, at the point of your decease or ill-health retirement. He said he couldn't see how that was possible. Such a decision would have to go through Management Board and the contents of the phone call could never be explained to members of MB and, in any case, if he let the Vice Chancellor know that he had recorded the call that was being used as evidence, all hell would break loose, he would virtually be committing career suicide. He said I was holding a gun to his head. I said that was true but that he had given me the gun, loaded it, and taken off the safety catch. Then I told him I had to leave. I gave him my card with my personal number and said he could call me that evening if he came up with a solution, otherwise I would see him in the morning at the hearing. Suddenly he wanted me to stay and talk but I left. He called me about two hours later. He said he had spoken to the University's lawyers and that he would be able to make a Compromise Agreement with you at the earliest possible opportunity. If we could postpone the grievance hearing he would negotiate the agreement with us before the end of the week. Employers use these agreements to sweep their dirty deeds under the carpet. They pay employees sums of money, often large sums of money, in return for their agreement to take no legal action against the employer for their employment hitherto and to keep all details of their prior employment confidential."

"You didn't say on the phone how much he agreed to pay," said Miller.

"That's still to be negotiated. And we need our lawyers to vet the draft agreement. But I told him that if he was considering a sum less than six figures then he could forget it. He said okay after a bit of a gulp. This process must be one he has some control over without referring to Covet, or if not he thinks he can finesse it somehow. Who cares? Hence why I am here now and not at the scheduled meeting. I am seeing him later this morning to get the ball rolling on the draft agreement."

"Good golly gosh, old boy!" Miller cried. "Spiffing! Christ, you fucked him ten times over!"

"Technically," said Redman, "it was Rachel Brace who did that. If she hadn't given me the recording from his phone..."

"Ahem," said Miller, altering his sitting position into one that seemed morally less comfortable. "Yes, Rachel. I'm afraid that on that score I have a bit of a confession to make. You see, I persuaded Rachel to give you the recording. She is retiring in a month, detests Asterisk utterly, is seething for revenge upon him, and there is nothing he can do any longer, even if he can prove her involvement, to harm her. He will suspect her, of course, because he gives her his phone all the time. He doesn't know how to install applications or updates and has her do it for him. But, ahem again, I'm afraid I lied to you a little. Rachel does not listen to his voice recordings and didn't know about this one. It was me who told her about it, who gave her the copy of it, and asked her to give it to you."

Redman was baffled. "I see. But how did you know about it?"

"James," Miller confessed, "I'm the Deputy Director of Information Services. I was the Director Elect. I have theoretical access to every piece of information on any piece of University hardware, mobile phones included. I can, technically speaking at least, read any email and listen to any call. It's largely not even legally dubious: in law, all this data is University property and I have licensed authority to control it. In the case of Asterisk and Covet, I know that they never put anything incriminating in writing. It's all done by phone. I simply installed a bit

29

of software in the telephony system that recorded every conversation made from each of their mobiles and landlines. We have security in place to detect such snooping but, being who I am, I was able to disable that."

"You had a *wiretap* up on their phones?" exclaimed Redman.

Miller shrugged. "I had been diagnosed with the big pancreatic C a fortnight before. When you know you are dying and are beyond the law you find yourself curiously free to do things you would never otherwise dream of doing. What can I say? I caught them in the act. I somehow thought they might do the dirty on me. But I wanted to ensure that they did not find out how I knew. That's where Rachel Brace comes in. If push comes to shove, she's prepared to take the rap. She too has nothing to lose and in some ways I think she'd like him to know she shafted him. They will think she simply took it off his phone and hopefully look no further. And, again hopefully, they will continue in the same vein, unawares, to record their dark secrets by phone."

"I see," said Redman. "Why *hopefully*?"

"Why, so that someone else can stop them, or nail them." Miller fished inside his dressing gown pocket. "I am hardly the only one they do this sort of thing to. You know that better than anyone. And you have been so good to me, James, so conscientious, so brave and resolute in many ways. It takes guts to do what you do. I was trying to think of some way to say thank you."

"Don't thank me. It's the Union, really. That's what gives me the authority."

"Well, the Union, then." Miller held up a USB thumb drive. "On this device are MP3s of all the recordings of conversations between Covet and Asterisk since early July: nearly three months of material. I don't understand it all, but you might. A lot of the personal references seem to be in code. For example, they always refer to me as *Loser*. But Asterisk screwed up in that call to Covet because he quoted the doctor using my real name. So I got what I needed from that one call. I didn't pay too much attention to the rest as I was too tired and none of it seemed pertinent and a lot of it I didn't understand. The executable file on this drive is the programme I used to make the recordings. It's configured so that, if it's installed on any University PC, the snooping cannot be detected by our internal data security. The calls are auto-recorded and downloaded to a secure off-site external server. You just choose your login details for that server and away you go. You are notified by email whenever a call has been recorded. Obviously you should not use your University email address for that. No traces are left on the hard disk of the machine itself on which the software is installed. It just acts as a transit point."

"Let me get this right," Redman asked incredulously. "You mean you are offering to let me *take over your wiretap*?"

"Not you. The Union, really. It may not be Watergate, old boy, but still, it could be one hell of a ride!"

Chapter Three

20 September

Most professional workplaces are, in essence, the sum of their conversations. Actions taken are often outnumbered by words spoken by hundreds of thousands to one. In a twenty-first century university, this ratio is more extreme than almost anywhere else, especially in view of the fact that the actions taken there often consist of little more than going and speaking, or sometimes writing, even more words to other, more people. This is exaggeratedly the case in faculties of Arts and Humanities, in which hardly any non-linguistic actions are ever taken at all. The denizens of these university corridors are primarily engaged in activities to be located somewhere within an algebraic continuum in which q speaks to r to entreat her to persuade s to have a word with t about an overlooked document written by u that should have been revised by v with subsequent approval by w (and is so approved after w has emailed v a reminder about it), who then forwards it to x, who will review and further endorse it (after having spoken testily on the telephone to w about v's tardiness and affectionately over coffee to u to inform her that she will ignore w's approval of v's incompetent revisions), letting y know, who will confirm to z that he can report the approval to q who makes p aware of the outcome; p then complains to o about how long all this has taken and the fact that the final approved document is not really what she was hoping for, namely v's revised text that w was kind enough to have shown her recently and said he had approved; o then tells n that p is complaining in her usual way, as she does about everything, and n reports confidentially to p that o is having a dig at her again, as she does at every opportunity. And so on.

At exactly the moment Buckrack finished delivering his valedictory and half minatory "Then you don't know who I am" to Asterisk, and Redman was staring in disbelief at the USB stick in Miller's outreaching hand, which he thought may already be a criminal item but knew would certainly become one if he took it and used it, the conversational baton was in danger of flying through a silent lapse of wordless air. But it was immediately caught and carried forward by Avril Poon, Associate Professor in the Department of Cultural Studies, and Sergei Krokoff, an improbably Ukrainian Professor in the School of English Studies. They had convened by appointment in the cramped space of room D4(b), which was Poon's office, and was in the same west wing of the Trump Building as Asterisk's more commodious quarters, but three floors higher up.

"This needs to be a conversation private," Krokoff began. "I would not want colleagues to know of. Not anyways right now."

"Okay," said Poon.

"I have problem," Krokoff went on. "With female graduate student."

Poon's deep brown eyes revealed themselves to him across the top rim of her glasses. "You don't say, Sergei," she said. "Would it be the first time?"

"Hah!" Krokoff exclaimed. "Is nothing improper. I think you think is hanky-panky or something. No. She is not nice girl, not Krokoff's type at all."

"I see," said Poon, but her eyes did not retreat behind her spectacles. "And if she *were* your type, Sergei?"

"No, she is not. Is dog. I mean, she is harmless puppy. You would know if you saw her."

"I wasn't asking *why* she is not your type, Sergei. I was asking *what if* she were your type?"

"Avril!" This was said with a long extension of the opening vowel: *Aaaavril*. The tone was one of wounded innocence. "You are going all feministical on poor Krokoff. I understand. Is not necessary. I am not here because you are President of Union and I have got myself in hot bath. Is academic matter."

Poon reclined a little in her chair and put her eyes back behind glass. "Okay. Go on."

"But has bit of embarrassing confession in it. That's why just between you and me."

"I understand, Sergei. Do please explain."

"Okay." Krokoff hunched forward and put his fingertips together. "Let us call this student Jane."

"Does she not have a name of her own?"

Krokoff knotted his brows. "Yes, is Jane. I said just now."

Poon sighed. "Okay!"

"Something is wrong with name Jane?"

"No! For goodness sake, Krokoff, get on with it!"

"Okay. Now this student, name Jane, she comes here from America with good, effective, first notch B.A., so good she win research scholarship, Vice Chancellor's Award, not even any need for Masters. Her Ph.D. proposal is right up my road, on the importance of 'things not said' in English novel. Narratology, very much a bag of mine. The proposal mostly about the Brontës but it also has legs, can spread. So like me you are thinking *Wuthering Heights*, how whole plot of book in fact cannot happen unless characters fail importantly to tell other people things crucial you or I would tell each other in real world most probable. So like Nelly Dean, who readers think insignificant character, just housekeeper, she is always choosing not to tell – "

"Sergei!" Poon intervened impatiently. "I get it. She had a research topic for which you were the appropriate supervisor. So?"

"Righto it is. So she arrives in January this year. We talk. Her initial idea is that her first chapter needs to be about 'things not said' generally before she gets to 'things not said' particular. She wants to write chapter about 'things not said' and their whole big cultural and social importance kind of thing. Even says fantastical-like that she is reaching for an overreaching philosophical 'theory-of-the-not-said'. I encourage her, thinking can always bring her down the line later, and the time was good for me besides as I was only half-way through *Villette* anyways myself, looking for the not said things."

"You are sure she said this to you, Sergei? Are you sure she didn't *not* say it to you?"

Krokoff closed one eye a little and cocked his head. "You joke me, right? You said say-not-say joke at me, right?"

Poon smiled patiently. "I did. Forgive me."

"I will. But is true there was thing she should have said she did not say which is what has caused me all my mad grief I am about to spill."

He paused. Poon rested her cheek on her right fist.

"Student name Jane watches TV," said Krokoff.

"TV?" Poon repeated. "She watches TV?"

"No! I mean, what does Krokoff care, what does anyone give a damn if she watches TV in private, even if she is addict of thing? As long as she keeps it to herself, righto it is?"

Poon rubbed her brow with two fingertips. "Sergei, you are speaking to a member of the Cultural Studies department. Do you expect me to agree with some narrow-minded, old fashioned literary critical view that television is an entirely negligible object of study? From what you say it sounds like she came back and wanted to do something with TV? Is that it?"

"Big time, massive time! When she came back after Easter all theory-talk had been chucked out of window into trash area. The Brontës had been lined up against media studies wall and shot through head with one bullet fired from the side, probably Anne first, bullet travelling so fast it went through all the Brontë skulls one after the other, not even the dignity of any ammo wasted on them individual-like, just a kind of instant economy genocide of the Brontës situation." Krokoff leaned forward and patted the palm of his hand on the desk for every word of his next sentence. "The - girl - had – got - *Lost!*"

There was a silence.

Buckrack was strolling around the campus grounds.

Redman was driving back from Miller's.

"Lost?" Poon said. "Lost in what? Lost where?"

"No, *Lost!*" cried Krokoff. "By her own confession, her bloody girlfriend turned her on. I think she must be a bit like you are, Sapphisticated, to be honest, and forgive me for throwing it up. The girlfriend introduced it into her. She had been missing supervisions with me to watch with girlfriend the whole six seasons of the goddamnit thing."

"*Lost?* You mean the American TV series?"

"Yes, and you can guess the next episode. Oh, oh, *Lost* had more things not said that should have been said than the dead, killed Brontës had to not say, it did, didn't it? One hundred and fifty chapters full of, or maybe I think empty with, things people should have told people but stupidly failed to do. Every singular character a Nelly Dean on steroidals. A far more fertile enquiry bucket than the three assassinated sisters, oh yes, and theory, oh, oh, that went swilling down the toilet soup bowl right after they did too, of course it did, did it not? Her entire Ph.D. thesis was now wanted to be about *Lost*!"

Poon contained herself. "And?"

"Well, what had she done, right? She had torrent-bitted the whole thing and she reached in her bag and put on my desk a USB finger drive with the entire nest of illegal data vipers on it and said I'd need to watch it."

"And you did what?"

"I looked at it. Flash drive gave me flashback. My first night in Budapest, I am walking along main street to my hotel when pretty girl, very pretty girl in tweedies and Sherlock Holmes deerstocking on her head comes up and gives me good card and says, all her many eyelids fluttering, in ridiculous broked-up English, *Naked ladies dancing on tables without bras.* Dot dotty dot. I was being pimped up. I was being offered illegal things by sly kind of temptress."

"And what did you do?"

Krokoff blushed. "Was many years ago," he said.

"I *mean,*" Poon leaned forward, "what did you do when *the student* offered you the USB stick with the bit-torrented TV series on it?"

"Well, it sat there for a moment, like some drug Krokoff had never had a try-out with. I don't even have TV." He looked guiltily aside. "They say *just say no*, but is not that easy when you're offered it blatant, right there, on top of your office desk, free, no questions asked, bam-wham."

"You took it?"

"Was persuaded."

"Then what?"

Reluctantly, Krokoff replied, "Gave it a go-try."

"I thought you didn't have a TV?"

Krokoff blushed anew. "I told her that. She made me stick it straight into USB slit of desktop PC right there in my office. Copied all the files onto hard drive. Showed me how to look into them. Took five bare minutes."

Poon contemplated him for a few seconds. "Is that it? You're worried about having illegal video files on your University PC hard drive?"

"God in heaven, no! I am Ukrainian! Breaking flimsy laws is not problem!"

"Then what, Sergei?"

"This is where you get to confession. Shamefulest part. But let me speak, I need to say. It all starts with Korean lady actress. Her name in *Lost* is Sun, which in English means centre of universe, probably means pretty orchid or some tritey sentimental nonsense in Korean, but soon this pretty orchid becomes centre of Krokoff's universe. They say Ukrainian girls are most beautiful in world, well, that's not true if you have go in Budapest, but really, in depth of soul, Krokoff has Asian persuasion and not caucasian orientation. I had cousin from Kazakhstan and she was first love of Krokoff at fourteen years of old, and this Korean lady, though eyes very different, and much more nicely breasted, she remind Krokoff very much of lovely Kazakh cousin, but more virtuous, less of tart, a devoted married lady. Her husband cannot speak English so he obviously cannot say nothing meaningful to anyone, excepting her. But worst shame of all, Korean lady Sun proves my wicked student name Jane right. She is biggest not-sayer of entire first two seasons. I mean, it goes without saying that nearly everybody in programme is choosing not to say important things they should be saying all the time if they had one quart common sense. Or they get prevented from saying them, like when Iraqi devil-angel Sayid gets struck on nut with log by someone (they don't say who) when he is trying to send radio SOS distress call. I mean, if he makes SOS message they all get rescued, righto, isn't it? So he's not allowed to say it. But Sun, silky desirable Korean lady, she actually secretly does speak English but she pretends she can't. And Krokoff knows this but other characters, even husband, do not, and this just doubles over and triples up her seductivity, because Krokoff shares her secret with her, and you get to watch her in long-lasting pictures of her pretty face, which you can make longer if you slow the motion up, when you know she is understanding what everyone else says but is deliberately not saying she understands, and so you get to imagine yourself on the island just with her, that's where Krokoff is in his head at those moments, everyone else has not got clue but she and Krokoff. But soon everyone has not said at least one important thing to everyone else, or they've said it to one and told them not to say it to others, and if everyone was only honest with everyone else and told them the complete truth they would have attained rescue by episode three of season one and it would be pointless village mini-series instead of sprawling metropolis maxi-epic. And some people are even not saying more than they are actually saying. But then Krokoff does not want them to achieve rescue anyways because he's staring with love and desire at the hot Sun. So Krokoff doesn't just notice that everyone is stupidly doing the not-said thing but soon he *wants* them to not say the sayable things because if they do say those things rescue plane will come and Sun will disappear over the horizon back to Seoul and sexy satin sheets with dumb fisherman husband. And sometimes Krokoff realises that he is feeling all this in his own University office at eight o'clock in the evening! And because he is doing all this naughty stuff on his University PC, between episodes it's easy to look up Wikipedia and other trashbags like, and so in no time at all Krokoff is rooting like a rat in the sewer internet looking for discarded bones for gnawing. And then the real horror movie in Krokoff's own head begins. He starts to cottonreel on to the intertexts, those repulsive post-modernist things. So when Sawyer says, 'I don't even wear cologne!' Krokoff finds himself laughing because he's been down in the sewer and seen there the advert for Davidoff Cool Water with the same male actor as the hunk model! Ho ho ho. But I might as well be laughing with a noose around my neck, because by the time I understand crap like that I too realise I am beyond rescue."

Krokoff stopped. Poon was staring at him, wide-eyed.

"You're not saying it," he said.

"I'm lost for words," she replied.

"Is no joke!" he exclaimed. "I am *Lost*! Is sewer juice running through Krokoff's veins. It gets worse!"

"Oh God!" Poon moaned.

"You have heard of Lostpedia?"

"No."

"Is garbage internet dustbin site for lost rats like Krokoff. There these rodents share their bubonic bones with one another. Like Wikipedia but more wicked, concentrated hydrochloric acid trivia just all about *Lost*. I have become dirty rat just like them. Diseased. Two days ago at midnight Krokoff made his first Lostpedia online contribution. Yesterday, high praise feedback from several other *Lost* vermin. I admit it. Am *Lost*aholic. Am addict. Avril, you need rescue me! You do TV shit in your department. Do it for me. Take this vile student name Jane and her potion from me!"

Poon adopted a pragmatic, sympathetic *mien*. "How deep are you in, Sergei?"

"Last quarter of season three."

"So three and a bit seasons to go?"

Krokoff nodded, sagging. "Will kill me. I swear, Krokoff will die if he does not get back to mainland soon."

"Are we talking full transfer of the student to this School? The entire student fee comes with her?"

"Anything! I am sure I can arrange."

"Have you spoken to the student?"

"Not yet. I've said nothing. For Krokoff, would be like waking up in bed with Hungarian whore. What does one say?"

"Best not to say anything, I suppose."

"You mean you will?"

"Is there something you're not telling me?"

"No! Unless you want Krokoff more humiliated than Krokoff is already."

"I mean anything important?"

"No. I swear on the life of student name Jane."

"Then send her an email and tell her to come and have a chat with me. But Krokoff, you're going to owe me one for this, once you've got your act together. "

"Ah, Avril, you are rock!"

Poon smiled drily. "Are we done?"

Chapter Four

20 September

Unlike the White House, the equally white Trump Building had a clock tower. Buckrack had disposed of his second histrionic cigarette while standing under it an hour before. And in this non-figurative, real ivory tower, an actual academic, almost mythically, had his office. It was a square cubicle just under the clock, accessed by a door off a winding staircase that led upward to the temporal machinery itself. The occupant's improbable name was Robert McNamara (no relation), and he was likewise strange. He had entirely lost the Galway accent of his childhood after his impoverished family moved to Glasgow on the day of his eighth birthday. Later, having decamped to Oxford for postgraduate study on the day of his twenty-first birthday, his acquired Glasgow brogue went through various Fabian metamorphoses so that he could be more easily understood by the uncomprehending middle class English students he met there. It would now have sounded quite refined to a Kelvinside ear, despite the fact that McNamara's only connection with Kelvinside had been his attendance at the University of Glasgow as an undergraduate, whence he returned each term-time weekday evening to his parent's mean tower block apartment in the north of the city. Indeed, he sounded these days just like all Caledonian BBC announcers, anglicised enough to be adored by the English, Scottish enough to be an object of pride to the Scots. When Irish students, or at least the Catholic ones, discovered he was actually Irish, they revered him also. Only the Welsh were not stirred somehow intimately by his person, and indeed the one individual in the University of Odium who hated him was a Welsh administrator to whom he had been in the habit of writing lacerating emails. Others, including his departmental colleagues, held him at a distance, thought him a troublemaker, were wary of the fact that he published about Marxism, sought to avoid his Irishy-Scottishy-unEnglishy habit of satirising those he considered fools and footlers with his council-house-*cum*-ivory-tower-vocabulary-boosted-tongue. But none disrespected him, because he had the reputation, in the nine years he had been President of the academics' trades union, of being a man of unusual integrity and suitably socialistic moral virtue. Even senior managers, who had reason to find him and his fellow Union officers obnoxious in their stubborn resistance to their plans and stratagems, had a soft spot for him, the way a whore has for a virgin: he was what they had once been but knew they could never be again. Then suddenly, one day, to the astonishment of everyone, like someone in a Philip Larkin poem, and a bit like his more infamous namesake, McNamara had resigned his Union membership, reasons never given to anyone, and went into a kind of silent internal exile, even volunteering, when space was short in the School of Political Science, to take the only vacant room that remained in the Trump Building, a room far too confined, remote and lacking in ostentation for a full

Professor such as him, which no one else wanted, because hardly anyone ever went there, and which he wanted for precisely that reason.

Unusually, however, today – which was McNamara's fifty-ninth birthday – James Redman was there. He was looking at McNamara's broad back and broader waist. McNamara was gazing through the window, his bulk almost hiding its frame. Outside in the distance the city of Odium shimmered to the east in the full light of the late morning hour, and McNamara said, "There must be something better than this."

Redman replied, after a pause, "I thought you asked for this office, no?"

"Oh no," said McNamara, turning around and sitting down in an armchair opposite Redman. "I did not mean the office. I love the office. It suits my increasingly isolationist bent. I meant this political torpidity, this nothingness of a polity we are in, even this cipher of an institution we work for, this empty vessel, this whited sepulchre. But then everywhere else is probably the same, or worse."

"Well," Redman ventured, "I thought the isolation was your way out."

McNamara smiled wryly. "Isolation is a way *in*, James, never a way out."

"That's gnomic of you, Robert," Redman said. "You know, you often strike me as being like some weird Celtic version of Aung San Suu Kyi."

"Oh no!" said McNamara, this time more sharply. "By comparison she's a paragon of unwavering Asian persistence, like some feminine pacifist General Giap or even Ho Chi fucking Minh himself. Nothing like western inner turmoil me. I am here because I hate myself even more than I hate what's outside me."

44

Redman felt the need to say something at this outburst. He wanted to ask, of course, after McNamara's inner turmoil, and why he would hate himself, a man only one Welshman was known to hate. But he said, instead, "I meant, it's like you're under some kind of self-imposed house arrest here."

McNamara did not acknowledge the comparison. "I met her, you know. She was married to a fellow don at Wolfson, my Oxford college. I was there when she left and returned to Burma. I often saw her in the Senior Common Room. A woman of astonishing grace and a curious beauty, so imbued with some kind of ineffable resolve and vigorous purpose, despite a seeming deep sadness, that I never knew what to say to her except hello. She had a beautiful, winsome, never quite full smile. I used to eavesdrop on the conversations she had with others. She never put a word wrong, and was unceasingly courteous and kind. I also met Benazir Bhutto, who was in Oxford at the same time and who, by comparison, though sexier, seemed to me a hound from hell. Do you want another coffee?"

"Er, no thanks."

"Then what is it you do want, James? I've been improvising conversation while you sit there looking shifty. I sense my counsel is being sought. If it's Union stuff, you can fuck off. *That* kind of politics I have left behind. It did nothing but cause me grief and it will cause you grief too."

Redman stirred. "Someone has to do it, Robert."

"Yes," McNamara agreed, "but it doesn't have to be you."

"True. But for now it's me."

McNamara sighed. "It *is* fucking Union stuff, isn't it?"

"In a way," Redman said. "But only indirectly, and you don't need to know the details. It's more a moral matter. You could think of it more in terms of the ethics of revenge, if that's easier for you. That's what I wanted to seek your opinion about."

McNamara grunted. "If you put it like that, I am in danger of being interested. I thought, however, that Jesus Christ had the last word on the ethics of revenge two millennia past."

"And you, Robert," Redman said sceptically, "are a turner of the cheek, are you?"

"You know I'm not," McNamara said. "But I sense, under the guise of seeking my advice, you are in fact trying to tempt me into complicity in something I probably want no part of. What is it the guy says in *The Sopranos*? 'Just when I thought I was out, they pull me back in.' Is it now you doing that? Why aren't you having this conversation with scissors-sister Poon?"

"Actually, he's quoting *The Godfather Part III*."

"Really?" said McNamara. "I haven't seen that. I don't watch movies these days. TV series seem altogether more cinematic, fuller, more epic."

Redman shrugged and said, "Anyway, you judge." He removed Miller's USB drive from his pocket and placed it on the low table between them. "I was given this by a dying man this morning, a man who has nothing to lose, a man who was wronged and, being in a position in which moral obliquity had little meaning, took an unusually radical step to right the wrong. He was also uncommonly successful, and his delight at the outcome is probably a little obscene. I feel a bit like I've been handed a murder weapon, having witnessed how effective it is, and invited to try it myself."

"For God's sake, stop talking like a Poe character.

Who? Who was wronged? Who wronged him? How did he screw them over?"

"You don't, as I say, need the details. But he was wronged by Tweedledee and Tweedledum, and this drive contains recordings of all the telephone conversations between the twins since late July, which he obtained by... let's call it sheer cunning. One of them, the only one I've heard, is enough to get a member of the University's clinical staff disbarred from his profession tomorrow. There are a hundred and twenty three more."

McNamara's left forefinger was between his teeth and he was staring at Redman in some wonderment. "Jamesh, Jamesh, Jamesh." He shook his head slowly. "Thish ish impreshive." He laughed. "I must say, as the students used to say, *respect*."

"It just dropped into my lap."

"And?"

"I wanted to know what you thought."

"What I thought you should do with it?"

"Yes."

"Well, I find it hard to imagine you will resist the temptation to listen to what's on it."

"It's true. I am tempted."

"Of course you are."

"So?"

"So what? You don't need my permission."

"But I want to know what you would think of my doing that."

"Christ. Is this really a moral dilemma you want me to debate with you? Or are you asking me to caution you about the obvious risks? Or do you, dear boy, *actually hope for my encouragement*? What if I *simply don't care*?"

"I think it's unlikely that you don't care, Robert."

McNamara looked over his glasses. "*Why* should I care?"

Redman shrugged. "Maybe you too are interested in revenge?"

McNamara stood up and walked to the coffee pot and poured himself another cup. "Ah, so it's not my better self you want to hear from, but a voice from my dark side? You've come, like Mephistopheles, to lure the soul of the good Dr Faustus into sin?"

Redman smiled. "I would merely like your spontaneous thoughts on the matter. My own, I admit, are confused. I'd like to test them against your touchstone. On the one hand, you know the people involved. You know the kinds of things they do. On the other hand, you've gone all Zen and seem rather detached these days from the kinds of passions these things stir up when you're still in the trenches, like me."

McNamara frowned. "I really do not know why you are issuing all these unlikely Asiatic analogies for my current choice of circumstances. I assure you there is nothing so profound or enigmatic to be puzzled over. But let's review the options anyway. I assume the recordings were acquired by criminal means, yes?"

"Apparently not. The person who acquired them is technically authorised to handle this kind of data."

"But you are not. So your possession of them is what is criminal."

"At first I thought so. But I soon realised that if the data contains evidence of malpractice or malfeasance then I think the case could be made that they were given to me with a potential Public Interest Disclosure in mind. I was given them in my capacity as a Union officer, in the course of Union business, and the Union has made PIDs in the past. I also know that at least one of the recordings – the one I heard before I knew of the others' existence, and which I got from another source – would easily merit a PID."

"So far so good. Then you can go ahead and listen, no?"

"I can plot the graph along the x-axis of the law. You're right. It's more the y-axis of morality I am having trouble with."

"Ethics?" McNamara snorted. "Honestly, James, you and your Cambridge notions. What is this, Industrial Conflict *versus* The Good Life?"

"There are more things in heaven and earth, Robert," Redman quoted. But still he eyed the USB stick on the table, matt black and self-contained, full of mystery and promise, like a miniaturised Kubrickian monolith.

"I see you," said McNamara, "looking at that thing the way one ogles a belly dancer in an Egyptian restaurant. One wants to reach out and – "

"Well, exactly," Redman agreed.

"Then," said McNamara, "take the advice you came to get. Let the sun go down on your curiosity. Sleep on it. That usually works for most people."

"It's a good idea," Redman said. "But can I leave it with you? If I don't – "

"Oh, I see. You fear you won't be able to resist the big trade Union deputy president hard-on it's giving you?"

"I *know* I won't," Redman confessed.

"So your virtue is actually no more laudable than the gap between a nicotine addict's smokes?" McNamara smiled. "It's actually restraint you are asking me to impose, not a call to conscience and duty? A sort of *hide my fags from me, will you?*"

"If you like."

McNamara gave a sigh. "Well, I guess if you do take a belly dancer home with you at night only one thing is likely to happen. No skin off my nose, I suppose. Tomorrow, coffee, noon, in the *Stern am Rathaus* downstairs? You can have it back then."

"Okay."

There was a short pause.

"Is there something else?" McNamara enquired.

"No," said Redman. "But, what, you're kicking me out? You want me to leave? Doctor's appointment over?"

McNamara looked surprised. "No. But I thought you said you had to see Tweedledum and be the monstrous crow."

Redman took out his phone and checked the time. "I have ten minutes."

"So," McNamara continued, "let's say you do listen to the recordings. Is there something you are hoping to find?"

Redman pondered. "Not particularly. The calls were all made over the summer recess. I'm actually surprised there are so many of them, but then Covet seems to be a shark who never sleeps. The one I heard was a nugget of gold in the personal case I was dealing with, but there has been nothing else of any moment, in the last couple of months, that I've had any inkling of. And unfortunately the nugget is going to be buried from the light of day once more in a Compromise Agreement. I expect the calls to reveal the usual war of attrition stuff, mind you, chipping away at the coalface here and there, as ever, but I don't have my ear to the ground on any major skulduggery. They use codenames, apparently. They called the person I was representing *Loser*. Ironic, really, as he's turned out the winner in this case. Well, sort of."

"I do not hesitate to point out," McNamara said, "that *Tweedledum* and *Tweedledee* are also codenames."

"But less openly disparaging," Redman replied.

"I'm not sure about that," McNamara disagreed. "Just more literary, no? Pretty pejorative all the same."

"Then not used with an intent to conceal or deceive. I think that's the difference."

McNamara shrugged. "If you say so."

Redman sensed again that McNamara wanted to let the conversation fade, and decided to change the subject. "Did you know that Rachel Brace was retiring in a month?"

McNamara narrowed his eyes. "I did." Then, after a pause: "Given that she has been the belly dancer I've taken home most nights for the past year and a half."

Redman, after some seconds, gawped.

"You didn't know?" McNamara asked. "Then I am pleased. We have indeed been as discreet as we planned."

"But," Redman spluttered, "but – "

"Now, now, James, just because you think she's a granny, being the modest age you are, and seem to consider me some Zen monk, that's no reason to be so shocked. What lights my candle need not light yours."

"All I meant was," Redman recovered, "you've kept that close to your chest."

"I've kept myself close to Madam Brace's chest," McNamara winked lasciviously.

Redman blew out a breath of *gee-whizz* air, then ventured, "Has she been... confidential?"

"You mean," said McNamara, "has she confided Tweedledum's secrets to me or has she kept his secrets?

You want to know if she's been my cochlear implant in his inner ear?"

"Well, yes."

"No. I told her I wanted to know nothing. It was easier that way for both of us plus, after I resigned the Union presidency, I genuinely wanted to know nothing. I've been more interested in Rachel's gyrating navel, if you get my drift."

"Please," said Redman, "spare me the geriatric images. But, then, you don't know?"

"Know what?"

"That it was Rachel who gave me the recording from Asterisk's phone? What I mean is, she pretended to give me the recording from his phone, because... Christ!" He gulped. "She must know! She must know about these recordings of Miller's! It was Miller who persuaded her to take the blame for divulging the recording that won the case I am going downstairs to see Asterisk about."

"Yes," said McNamara, "I did know about that. When Miller approached her she asked me what I thought she should do. Rachel has hated Asterisk pretty much forever. But Miller only talked to her about one recording, the one you've heard. No doubt he did not want her to know as much as you now do. After all, what would she do with knowledge that he had a total treasure trove of telephone tittle-tattle?"

"She never asked him where he got it from?"

"Of course she did. He told her he made it himself but that if he was known as the source his case would be potentially impossible to win because of the possible criminal dimension. Even though he's dying he *did* have something to lose: his case, the settlement, all that cash. But because she was retiring *she* had nothing much to lose *and* something to gain. And so we get back to revenge: her revenge on Tweedledum. Her chance to be the monstrous crow."

"But," Redman was still incredulous and a little hurt, "why didn't you tell me?"

"Well, firstly, she forbade me. But surely it's obvious, James? It was a tactic. You couldn't know 'til after you had won the case. You walked into your meeting with Asterisk yesterday believing the recording had been obtained by whistleblower Rachel – someone other than Miller. You thus acted with a clear conscience on his behalf and with her seeming permission. Had you known that Miller was the source, and that he'd pulled it out of his superabundant lucky bag of devious recordings, you might have baulked. Everyone knows how proper you are."

Redman looked appalled. "But I feel manipulated. Like I've got your hand stuffed up my arse."

"*My* hand? What did I do? I simply did not tell you something I had been forbidden to tell you. If anyone's hand was up your arse it was Miller's, while his other hand's been knock knock knockin' on heaven's door. What, you're going to hold a dying man to some supreme standard of verity, when he's trying to get compensation for what he's been diddled out of, a nest-egg to leave behind for his wife and kids, a reseizure of the plunder that's been illegally stolen from him by those two malevolent pirates? You expect a man drowning in the cancer tank to play by the rules of the game? You expect him to go down like the *Loser* they called him? Rachel did the right thing, a final favour to him. You did the right thing, you went into the ring for him when they knocked him down and you KO'd the bastards with the leaden gloves he gave you. You won. How often did we ever really beat them, James? And not only that, but now you have the spoils of war: the other recordings. You might be able to cause even merrier hell with them."

There was a substantial silence.

Redman eventually stirred. "So you knew about Miller and Rachel, but you didn't know about the other recordings?"

McNamara shook his head. "Not 'til you came in here today with them. Miller didn't tell Rachel about them. So she couldn't tell me about them. And she made me swear not to tell you about her and Miller's stratagem."

"But here am I," Redman said, "telling you about them."

McNamara nodded. "Yes. But you needn't have."

"But I did. I wanted your advice."

"I gave you my advice. Sleep on it. We'll talk about them more tomorrow."

Redman stood up. He was trying to contain his anger and failing. "But now," he said, "now I know the truth and I have to go downstairs and lie to Asterisk."

"You knew the truth before you came in here to see me this morning," McNamara replied. "You knew more than I did. A couple of pieces of the jigsaw had been withheld from you, that's all. You were still going to go into Asterisk's office, knowing what you did, and take him for all you can get. And I'm sure that is still what you will do. I can't imagine you will throw the case overboard in an epileptic spasm of probity just because you were kept a little in the dark."

"No." Redman walked to the door. "I won't." He relaxed a little as he stopped on the threshold, but seemed still dismayed. "Yet I feel like a pawn on a chess board."

"More a rook, I think," said McNamara, and then, after a moment, added: "A monstrous crow."

PART TWO
24 OCTOBER – 25 OCTOBER

Chapter Five

24 October

Rachel Brace, the sheet of McNamara's double bed tucked under her armpits because an unexamined prejudice suggests that readers probably do not seek a visual description of naked sixty year-old breasts, looked longingly across at the man who had, half an hour before, given her a semi-vigorous seeing to. "But why did you not tell me all this before?" she chided.

McNamara turned from the computer screen with its list of files. "For the same reason we never talked about any of it. Until today you were an employee of the University of Odium and I did not want to mix business with *etcetera*."

"But," protested Rachel, "that pretty much ended that day, when Asterisk kicked me out, or rather told me to take my last month as a holiday."

"All the same," McNamara replied. "Best to do these things properly."

"I guess," Rachel said.

"The thing I can't figure out," McNamara went on, "is why he seemed to accept your fairy tale that he had made the recording when he hadn't?"

"Because he does make lots of recordings. He just couldn't remember. He was also fuming and baying for my blood, and he only got worse when I gave it to him straight between the eyes and said the bloody phone call was illegal and outrageous and he deserved to be hung, drawn and quartered for it. My fake confession seemed to convince him that he had done it after all. He would have loved to sack me, I'm sure, but he obviously knew that was impossible, given the hand grenade I was holding."

"Leaving me to *sack* you," McNamara quipped cheesily, his eyes glinting.

"Uh-huh," Rachel responded invitingly.

"Later," he said. "I have to go out for half an hour."

"Shame," she said, then, pensively, "What I can't figure out is why he called me in about it after his meeting with Buckrack. What did Buckrack have to do with it? He'd only just arrived. Do the calls tell you anything about Buckrack?"

"Nope," said McNamara. "He's mentioned only twice. In late July Tweedledee calls Tweedledum and says, 'I had a long talk with a guy called Buckrack on the plane from LA the other day. Remind me to talk to you about him when we next meet.' The day before Buckrack appears he calls him again and says, 'Buckrack will turn up tomorrow morning. Act as instructed.' That's it, nothing more."

"I called Alison. She says Buckrack has been in three times to her knowledge, and every time it seems to freak Asterisk out. The last time, she said, he was positively shaking afterwards."

"Well, right up to the eve of Buckrack's arrival they are not using a codename for him, which is what they usually do when something nefarious is being discussed, or when they want to be plain insulting."

"And you?" Rachel asked. "What's your codename?"

"Why," said McNamara, "I am the *Secretary of*

Defense, of course. Which makes Covet LBJ and Asterisk Dean Rusk, or somebody. I think what they mean is that I should be on their side, being a Professor and all, but I have turned unexpectedly into some weird raving internal opposition. But they don't mention me much, and compared to the other codenames mine is pretty polite."

"E.g.?"

"Well," McNamara glanced at a written list on the desk. "Poon is known as *Bowling Ball.*"

Rachel looked puzzled. "*Bowling Ball?*"

"Yeah, you know, the way you put your middle finger..."

Rachel giggled. "That's pretty witty."

"Must be Covet's. Asterisk isn't clued up enough for that, though I wouldn't put it past him to find these things on the internet to try to impress Covet. She's also sometimes referred to as *Fajita Eater.* Miller, we know, was *Loser.*"

"Which just seems even crueller now that he's dead. They should fry in hell."

"Agreed. It took me some time to figure out that Redman was *Dr Watson*, because we actually have two real Dr Watsons on the staff, one of them, believe it or not, in the actual Medical School, which is a hoot."

"It's not entirely insulting, is it?" Rachel mused. "I mean Watson is a good guy, no?"

"Perhaps the suggestion is that he is rather limited compared to Holmes. Needless to say, there's no *Sherlock.*"

"No," Rachel said. "But then I suppose you've staked a claim to that name yourself now, no?"

"How'd you mean?"

"Well, destroying the USB stick he gave you, but copying it first and poring over its contents these last few weeks. James must have been furious."

"He was. Though I think I convinced him it was for his own protection."

"But Robert," said Rachel, moving her pillows and sitting up, though not enough to reveal presumably withered nipples, "what gave you the right? Were you not stealing his scoop as well?"

"Right?" McNamara grumbled. "There's no right in any of this. It's all precisely *wrong*. Every one of them – Miller, Covet, Asterisk, even you, perhaps, and ultimately James as well – all acted in the *wrong*. It's what this place has become. It's like a little city in which the only order possible is created by everyone committing crimes which cancel the others' crimes out. When James came to me with the recordings he was talking precisely about *revenge*."

"Yes, but you didn't *destroy* the files, Robert. You copied them and lied to him. That was a wrong too."

"Yes," McNamara admitted, "it was. Still, it's like my father always said: sometimes experience just needs to make the decision, without reasoning it out. You know about James's lack of *sangfroid*, how passionate he gets, how crusading, how all *Martin Luther-King* he can be. He'd have spent the last month being eaten up by these recordings, trying to decode them, planning a campaign around them, when what he really needs to do is write his book."

"So? Maybe that's what's needed. Maybe there's too much *sangfroid* in the veins of this place."

"But people exploit his goodness all the time, Rachel. It's exactly what Miller did, setting the whole thing up via you. And that turned it to wrongness."

"But the end was good, no?"

"It was good for Miller. Or good for his family, I mean. I don't see how it was good for James. All it did was make him even more the enemy of Tweedledum."

"I disagree," said Rachel. "Those recordings would have strengthened his arm, not weakened it. Yet you took them off him."

"Strength is not the same as right," McNamara sighed. "But let's not argue. I could give them back to him anytime. I just see no need to. From what I've heard it's all gossip and nastiness and effing and blinding. What's new? We could have guessed they did that anyway. It's exactly what *we* do." He stood up. "I have to go over to the Hall. A Hall Tutor wants to see me about something. You'll stay?"

"I was promised an *I am boss* night. I get to use you entirely for my selfish pleasure."

McNamara smiled wryly. "That's correct."

"I'll be here," Rachel said.

It had once been called Barraclough Hall of Residence, after a minor aristocratic family in a neighbouring county, in the days when such appellations were considered to lend weight and dignity to provincial institutions. But two years previously it had been renamed Coolwipe Hall, in honour of the sponsorship of the Coolwipe Toilet Hygiene Company, which had its world headquarters in Odium. A study had been done. With thirty-six thousand students and six thousand staff, the University consumed (including thefts) approximately fourteen hundred toilet rolls per day during term. The annual cost was estimated at over a hundred and fifty thousand pounds *per annum*. Coolwipe's offer to partner with its local university by supplying it, free for a five-year period, with its revolutionary Moisture Tissues (impregnated with aloe vera and camomile) resulted in an annual advantage of over two hundred and thirty thousand pounds, once the savings and price differential with ordinary toilet paper had been factored in. This seemed cheap at the price of merely a new sign over the door of the erstwhile Barraclough Hall and some relatively tasteful green floral logos in lavatory dispensers.

There had been a time when McNamara might have poked fun at such a decision in committee. He had been tempted to suggest that the new name be "Fresharse Hall", partly because a few like-minded critics round the table would have acknowledged and enjoyed the pun. But, to everyone's surprise, he had acquiesced without comment. It had become difficult to argue against such a move. While it meant that henceforth he would be the Warden of a Hall of Residence whose name ineluctably reminded one of clean-up operations subsequent to evacuation, it saved money and the new tissues were unarguably a luxury compared to the frictive industrial grade scrolls which had preceded them. The absorbency of the latter was questionable and their caustic effect on haemorrhoids was undoubted. Thefts rocketed, because even the staff now purloined Coolwipes, which was why the dispensers were hermetically sealed and only one tissue at a time was released. It was plain to everyone who Coolwiped (a new verb around campus) that there was no going back after doing so: parched recycled chemically bleached paper would not be allowed anywhere near the anuses of generations of Odium alumni again. The company had offered the University an advantageous deal at the expiry of the free five-year period. But by that time, McNamara had it on good authority, the University would be looking to trade up, at a new sponsor's even greater expense, to hi-tech Japanese hydro-toilets with integrated blow-dryers.

In any case, Coolwipe Hall of Residence was way down the pecking order of sponsorship, at the bottom in reality as well as figuratively. It was a squat cuboid of 1965 concrete slabbery built on reclaimed marshland near the campus's western perimeter. From the front it looked like an enormous grey and brown shoebox with a copper lid gone green from decades of rainfall. It was not the ugliest residence on campus. In 1966, when higher education in the United Kingdom was still organised along what one could tenably call a Soviet system (accepting only élite cadets and each year turning out cadres of well-educated, market-unfriendly graduates) the University Grants Committee issued an edict that no further capital allocation would be made to subsidise University Halls of Residence after December of that year. Odium did not have time to commission plans for a new hall, so it took the recently completed blueprints for Barraclough, turned them through one hundred and eighty degrees, and built the virtually identical Wykenshawe (now Boxitgood) Hall down the hill at its rear. Thus Coolwipe was the joint ugliest residence on campus and, with its near twin, could enjoy only modest expectations of patronage. At the top of the pyramid was Powell Hall, the only one of the fifteen Odium residences which retained a human designation, the University's one attempt to create something that looked architecturally like an Oxbridge College. It seemed forever immune to having its original name blown away by the cyclones of twenty-first century commerce, as it was already endowed by the estate of a dead Conservative Cabinet member of eld whose private largesse exceeded anything the world of trade might calculatedly muster. But all else was fair game, and those on slightly lower rungs even attracted titles which advertised multinational companies. Toyota Hall stood adjacent to the Toyota

Engineering Building, which was why the Vice Chancellor's chauffeur-driven limousine was a Lexus. Adobe Hall, near the Adobe Computer Laboratory, had even had its façade renovated to make it look as if it were built from brown mud.

None of this was in McNamara's mind as he walked the hundred metres from his house to a door at the car park end of Coolwipe still marked "Trade Representatives' Entrance". Nor did he on this occasion reflect ironically, as he had often done in the past, that this sign might these days truthfully be posted on virtually every main entrance on the Odium campus, and not just those out of ordinary sight. Instead, as he paused before entering to pop half a Viagra in anticipation of his return to Rachel, he was thinking of the unusual pleasure of their etiolated love. He knew that the young, including himself when young, would have scoffed at overhearing their private dirty talk, perhaps even been repulsed by their overweight congress, their weak libidinal wheezes, clicking joints, and paltry moans and groans. But the young would never understand, unless they were lucky enough to meet someone in later life who accepted their own and their bedfellow's growing physical frailty, that accommodation to the relentless decline of the body could take on the form of renewed mutual ex-perimentation. The truth was that the tongue and the mouth were not as prone to dystrophy as the penis was to dysfunction and the vagina to slackness. The clitoris remained a taut, responsive miracle, the frenulum as excitable a piece of small tissue as it ever had been. Once a couple abandoned the illusion that sexual success consisted mainly in simultaneous climaxes involving a glorious engorgement within tightly clutching labia, there was a whole new world of blissful pampering of one another to discover. If one added the fact that contraception was no longer a matter to regard, and the psychologically stimulating insight that you were both building an empire of the senses from which the rest of the world assumed you had been exiled long ago, the possibility of regular thrills seemed unlimited.

It was because of these thoughts, having walked along an internal corridor and down a set of steps to the bunker-like Senior Common Room and entered, that McNamara did not register what to any man less preoccupied would have been the blatantly powerful sexual radiation which constitutionally emanated from Jane Blake. To be sure, even he could not fail, at each sighting of her, to make a rapid venereal appraisal. There was the wonderful head of full-bodied brown hair tumbling to halfway down her back, the large brown Hispanic eyes, the plump but well-shaped lips, the perfectly formed nose, the beautiful complexion unadorned by make-up, and below the neck the 115-pound figure, accentuated usually by tight-fitting clothes, which amply displayed a fine, round but not too big behind, and anti-gravitational 34B breasts, with legs that went three or four inches higher than his own before meeting slim bracket-shaped hips and a proportionately thin waist. She was undoubtedly neat whisky to Rachel Brace's diluted beer. McNamara thought, as he always thought the moment he saw her anew, that male undergraduates must pretty well instantly cream their pants when introduced to her as their Hall Tutor. But no such ripple broke within his own self, he did not feel a snapping pang of immediate regret that no part of his own anatomy would ever come nearer to Jane's than the hand with which he shook hers. Even had he possessed a wooden horse, he would not have wished to force it through her gates of Troy. For he had discovered, with Rachel, that libidinal weakness was also great source of moral strength. It allowed him to look at Jane almost entirely aesthetically, the way a proper father might look at his objectively gorgeous daughter. Rachel made him happy. She was not even the mast to which he tied himself to resist the sirens on the shore. With her, there simply was no shore, just open sea.

Jane seemed to McNamara entirely aware of the adrenalin-inducing tendencies of her being, and while she did not dress to mitigate them, her faultless propriety of conduct seemed calculated to deflect them. Thus the handshake in which she curiously indulged at the opening of nearly every meeting. To be sure, her east coast Sweet Valley High accent destroyed instantly any illusion that she might be some latterday exemplar of Jane Austenish containment and reserve. But she also used, without apology and despite regular dis-couragement, formal titles instead of first names: "Good evening, Professor McNamara." She never flirted. McNamara had seen others flirt with her, and she always responded to them with studied, even marked, emotional neutrality. Her consistent comportment seemed, over time, to be a polite notice to the excited male: please detumesce. But despite her faultless and chastening manners, women tended to hate her. On the whole, on balance, McNamara quite liked her, although he did not think of her much except when they met in person. It was perhaps because of this that she seemed more comfortable with him than she often was with others.

They indulged in the customary small talk about the start of the new academic year and the fresh intake of students, and McNamara enquired routinely about progress on her Ph.D. without listening much to the answer. Jane asked cordially after his family, his two sons, whom she had never met. She smoothed her mid-length black skirt under her thighs with the palms of her hands and sat down decorously on one of the sofas.

"What did you want to see me about?" McNamara asked, taking a seat opposite her, about six feet away.

She appeared nervous. "It's not easy to talk about. I hope you won't mind. It's not about the Hall."

"Okay," he said. He was impatient to return to Rachel but determined to try not to show it.

He was not expecting her to say, "Professor McNamara, are you a person of faith?" And it startled him when she did.

Although his eyebrows raised involuntarily, he shrugged his shoulders to relieve himself of the surprise. "No," he said, "but I was raised a Catholic."

She smiled. She had a symmetrical, natural smile, and flawless American teeth. "I guessed," she replied. "With a name like yours. Me too. But I am a believer."

McNamara smiled gently, crookedly back. "And?"

She hesitated. "I am having something of a crisis, I think."

McNamara felt he also ought to wait a second or two before replying, "A crisis of faith?"

"No," she blurted. "I have been... sinful... of late."

McNamara drew in a heavy breath. "Isn't that more the kind of thing you would talk to a priest about?" he said.

"Yes," she said. "I would. I mean, I shall. But it's more complicated."

"How?"

"It's embarrassing as well as... spiritually comprom-ising."

"Okay," he said patiently. "We are confidential here, obviously."

"Yes," she said. "Thank you."

There was another lull. McNamara broke it. "Tell me more only if you feel you need to," he cautioned, hoping privately that the caution might be acted upon.

"I want to tell someone," she replied. "It's got to that stage."

"Okay," he said.

"I've..." He could see that she was biting her lower lip. She continued, "I've become involved with a member of staff."

"Ah." McNamara held up his hand, somewhat off-iciously, he thought. "Before you go on, whether or not this matters, can I just give you the low down on this kind of thing, from the University's point of view? Sin is not a category of offence the University concerns itself with. Relationships between students and staff are assumed to be private matters of adult consent unless there is a conflict of interest or you are under eighteen or deemed to be a vulnerable person. You are neither, I am sure, and the only avoidable conflict of interest would be with someone who assesses your work. Even then, all that needs to happen is that the conflict of interest is removed by ensuring the member of staff does not assess your work. If you are worried that you're doing something wrong, then you're not, unless the member of staff supervises you... and, well, that's unlikely to be the case, right?"

Jane put her fingers to her teeth. She was too careful about her fingernails actually to bite them, but she worried at them for a moment or two. "Yes, I did look at the regulations," she said. "I am not so bothered about those. I'm more concerned with the sinfulness of it."

McNamara looked over his glasses at her. "Is this because you already have a boyfriend?"

"No," Jane said. "It's not a matter of infidelity. It's the nature of the... new relationship."

McNamara pondered. "I understand. These things can become difficult. The member of staff, is he married?"

"No," she said. "And it's not a man."

There was yet another, this time longer, hiatus. McNamara took off his glasses and rubbed his brow with his fingers.

"Oh Lord, indeed," he said. "Okay. Can we leave the sin thing aside for a moment and just deal with the conflict of interest issue? There's no conflict of interest, right?"

Jane was silent. She remained so.

McNamara sat up. "Dr Poon?" he said, more loudly than he meant to. "You're having a sexual relationship with your supervisor?"

Jane hung her head and looked down at her shoes.

"Aw, Jesus!" he exclaimed.

Jane glanced up. "Please, Professor McNamara."

He caught himself. "Sorry," he said. He stood and walked to the window and thought for a moment. "Well, tell me what you feel like telling me." He turned and sat down again and listened.

She made to begin, but he cut her off. For some reason he found himself now instantly in listen-to-me-young-lady mode, as if she really were his daughter. "What are you thinking, Jane? You're not gay. Poon's been shacked up with another woman in Bigton going on ten years. She's old enough to be your mother. You manage well enough to dispose of the attentions of numerous young men around here, so what happened on this occasion? Oh, hell, don't start crying!"

"I'm sorry," she sniffed. "I know it's hard not to judge me. But I judge myself, believe me. I know it's wrong. I can deal with men. Maybe it's because she's not a man that it was different this time. I tried to break it off."

McNamara had always been unimpressed by student waterworks. They did not soften his heart, but hardened it.

"And?" he demanded.

"She said she missed me terribly. She pleaded with me and I went back to her. I don't know why, but this isn't like being with a man. She says she loves me. If I'm honest I missed her too."

"Jesus Christ!" he exclaimed, then he sighed, and subsided. He apologised again. "I'm sorry. Look, why tell me? What do you want from me?"

She said, half questioningly, "You seem to know how things work around here. And I know you know her personally."

"Advice, then?" he said. "First of all, let's be practical. Review the options. You can continue, but she has to stop being your supervisor. You can end the relationship with her, and even then you cannot really go on being supervised by her. But she should already have told you that."

"She said if I stopped seeing her she'd be suicidal. It's like emotional blackmail. I've already changed supervisor once. How can I do it again? It begins to look suspicious."

"You mean Krokoff? Can't you go back to being supervised by him?"

"No," she shivered. "He's disgusting. To be honest, he was coming on strong. I changed my subject partly to get away from him. That's why I'm with Dr Poon now, which involved an entire transfer from one department to another in a different School. And that was only a month or so ago. What is it going to look like if I ask to change again?"

McNamara looked at her with some pity. "The only

70

other option is to make a formal complaint against her, and the matter will be resolved by someone else, but I assume you don't feel that way."

"But how can I do that?" she said. "I don't want people to know about it. And I don't want to criticise her. She did harass me into it, it's true. But I did consent. I wasn't forced." Suddenly she looked frightened. "You said we were confidential, right? You're not going to tell anyone, are you? You're not going to talk to Dr Poon? She'd go crazy if she knew I had told you. She said we had to be very discreet."

McNamara considered. "No," he said. "But if you didn't want anyone to know perhaps you should not have told me either. I understand why you wanted to speak to someone, but you don't seem to want to entertain the only possible solutions. You could see a University Counsellor. It's free. You just call and make an appointment. It might do some good to talk it through with them, at least the, er, spiritual issues. Or your priest, of course, if that works for you. The practical issues are as I described them."

Jane dried her eyes. "Yes," she said. "Maybe that's a good idea. If I do that I might get some perspective on it."

"All right," he said. "Tell you what. You do that and then if you want to talk again we can. You're clearly in a bit of a pickle but I'm sure, if you give it some time, that it might work itself out in your mind."

Jane stood up and looked at him with gratitude. "Professor McNamara, please don't be angry with me," she appealed. "I'm glad I spoke to you, and I'm sorry if I've put you in an awkward position. I didn't mean to. It was just depressing me awfully."

"No," he said. "And I am sorry if I was short with you. That was wrong of me. These things do take time to resolve."

Jane extended her hand formally in a way that young twenty-first century women hardly ever do.

In difference, similarity. Jane Blake tottered through Coolwipe Hall to her small apartment on the third floor, genuinely nervous and emotionally overwhelmed by the enormity of the confession she had just made. McNamara, on the other hand, thought little as he departed the Hall of the interview that had taken place. After three decades of working in universities, he had become accustomed to thinking he had heard it all, only once again to hear something novel. But there really was a Zen part of him. In the way that he treated all confidential matters, he discarded almost immediately the details Jane had told him, like a letter thrown in a postbox and forgotten unless it was returned to him again at a later date. He was more concerned with Rachel and tonight's promised sexual excess. He stopped on the way and brought to mind an anticipatory mental image that might indicate if the Viagra was kicking in, a fantasy touchstone that would help his lower half obey a certain bidding: please tumesce. Satisfied, he proceeded. When he entered the house, it was entirely in darkness. This was a game he and Rachel often played, a kind of phallic hide-and-seek. He found her in the downstairs bedroom, on a product placement Eames leather swivel chair, her legs spread with wonderful obscenity across its arms, pelvis bared and appropriate organ gaping. To the reader's likely relief, he did not turn on the light before beginning his demonic work on his willing, vocally consenting subject.

Jane also entered her flat, likewise, but for different reasons, excitable. By contrast, however, after locking her door, she turned on the light. And sitting in her modest lounge, also on a swivel chair, but one without a brand name, she found, though fully clothed, with his legs crossed, Buckrack.

"Hello, Jane," he said. "Me Tarzan."

Chapter Six

25 October

Early the following morning, before his secretaries arrived for work, Nigel Asterisk was eyeing Buckrack tremblingly across the desk in his office. This was quite literally so, as in the last few weeks his right eyelid had developed a twitch, which he had experienced before, but on this occasion he attributed it to the stress and worry the American kept regularly bringing his way. Buckrack looked impatient and, as usual, slightly contemptuous.

"Another one?" Asterisk said.

Buckrack sighed demonstratively. "The first three were listening devices. This is a pinhead wireless camera and a miniature video recorder. I need them quick. They do next day delivery, so make the call now."

"But *why*?"

"Well, obviously," Buckrack persevered, "because we need to see something as well as hear it."

"*We*?"

"I'm sure you know Covet has approved it."

"Yes, yes. But this, and another request for a building master key, the illicit entry and the nefarious surveillance..."

"Illicit? Nefarious? There's no law against an employer

monitoring his employees. These are corporate offices, not private residences."

"But why? It's extremely irregular."

"You don't need to know why. I would venture that you don't even want to know why."

Asterisk scratched his head. "I don't have deniability. These orders are being made on my budget with my authority. The Vice Chancellor made it very clear that that's how it should be done. I'd like to know at least a little of what's going on."

"You can ask Covet if you want to know *why*," countered Buckrack. Then he seemed to turn conciliatory. "But, since you asked, I'll tell you *what*. Okay?"

Asterisk nodded in anything-is-better-than-nothing agreement.

"The first three bugs, the ones I requested in the first week, went into the offices of Redman and Poon and McNamara, all in this building. When I asked for the two master keys a fortnight later it was so that I could remove the one from McNamara's office. No conversation ever seems to take place there. As far as I can tell, McNamara receives no visitors at all. He has only postgraduate research students and seems to conduct all his business in the Senior Common Room of the Hall where he is Warden, and if I had a pad that nice I'd do that too. So I planted it there instead. I am not about to tell you what we have gleaned so far. That would be premature and it's for Covet's ears only. But matters have sufficiently developed for me to judge that we also need a video feed from Poon's office. That's where most of the Union information flows through and where the executive committee meetings take place. But we need to know who is present at the meetings and the audio alone doesn't give us that."

Asterisk looked troubled. "So we are essentially monitoring the executive officers of the Union?"

"McNamara is not an officer."

"Not anymore. But he is the ex-President."

"He's not even a member these days. Word is he resigned lock, stock and barrel over a year ago."

"That I didn't know," said Asterisk. "But they probably seek his advice all the same. Poon's not plugged in the way McNamara was."

"Nope," said Buckrack. "On the evidence of the last month he hasn't had a single conversation with anyone about Union matters, and certainly not Redman or Poon."

"That's hard to believe. The man's a Marxist, you know. A meddler in management business for years, unlikely to change."

"Well, I thought the way you do at first, and we'll continue to keep tabs on him, but the signs so far are that there are no longer spots on this leopard."

Asterisk picked up the order information on the camera which Buckrack had written down for him. "And how long do we think we will go on doing this?"

Buckrack was non-committal. "As long as it takes."

"As long as it takes to find out *what*?"

"That's really a *why* question disguised as a *what* question. But you can imagine how important it is for management to know what the Union is discussing."

"Yes," Asterisk agreed. As an afterthought he asked, "You plant these devices at night, I assume?"

Buckrack nodded.

"My worry is," Asterisk confided, "that they might be discovered."

"That's unlikely," said Buckrack. "They're so micro they can hardly be found without special detection equipment. That's one of the reasons they are so expensive."

"But how do we use any information we learn from using them without it becoming obvious that we have?"

"Oh, there are ways," Buckrack reassured. "Don't you worry about that. Now put the camera order through today. I'll be back first thing in the morning to pick it up."

Asterisk examined the peremptory Buckrack steadily for a moment, but he could feel his eyelid beginning to tremble uncontrollably again, and averted his look. "You can get the master key from the security office," he said. "Tell them to call me to confirm."

Once Buckrack had departed, Asterisk's mind drifted to episode four of season six of *The West Wing*, which dramatised C. J. Cregg's first day as White House Chief of Staff after Leo McGarry's heart attack. C. J. was being undermined by that son of a bitch Secretary Hutchinson, who was taking advantage of her inexperience in the role to circumvent her and go directly to the President about weapons grade uranium in the Republic of Georgia. C. J. sat down with Margaret, her PA, and asked her for advice. Margaret told her she should go through her policy wonks. "Right," said C. J. "How many policy wonks work for me?" Margaret replied, "A bunch." In the last ten minutes of the episode C. J. gathered her policy wonks and swiftly reasserted her authority over Hutchinson without having to approach the President directly.

The problem, Asterisk pondered, was not just that he had no policy wonks or equivalent. He did not even have a PA such as Margaret. Indeed, Rachel Brace, on whose experience he had long depended, had committed a decisive act of final betrayal, and Alison Stilt was little more than an obedient-to-command know-nothing. But the deeper difficulty was that Buckrack was not as evidently surmountable as Secretary Hutchinson. He was Jack Bauer, he had virtually said so. Asterisk had in the last month taken out a free trial subscription to Netflix to acquaint himself with *24*, and watched it compulsively with intensifying horror. What became very clear very quickly was that Bauer would go round anyone to get directly to an honourable President like David Palmer, and if the President was a bad egg like Charles Logan he would ignore even his authority. There was much to be learned from episode six of season five, for example, in which Chief of Staff Walt Cummings first persuaded President Logan to curb Bauer's seemingly irrepressible activities only to suffer the terrifying consequences, in front of the President himself. "The first thing I'm gonna do, I'm gonna take out your right eye," Bauer had then threatened, brandishing a knife in Cummings' face. "Then I'm gonna move over and I'm gonna take out your left." The President had stood by, powerless to prevent him, as the blade almost cut into Cummings, until at the last moment he confessed to his crimes and was subsequently found dead, hanging from a rafter. The entire series had sent regular shivers of recognition down Asterisk's pliable vertebrae. The Vice Chancellor was not David Palmer. He was much more like Charles Logan. Asterisk himself did not want to be Walt Cummings. He wanted to be Leo McGarry, minus the heart attack and his own currently flickering right eyelid.

At around the same time, Jack Russell decided to show his dogged discontent by lying flat out on his stomach with his chin on his paws staring reproachfully at his human companion. The morning had in fact begun well. He had roused Redman, who seemed likely to sleep eighty per cent of the time if left to his own devices, and managed to orientate his easily distractable intelligence into donning the necessary gear required for a vigorous run into campus. He had manoeuvred him out of the front door by carefully persuasive body language and a politic lack of overt vocal insistence, so skilfully, in fact, that Redman probably believed he was acting on his own frisky agency. They had reached the front garden gate and were about to start trotting when another human emerged from a car parked at the pavement and stood in Redman's way. This was a much fatter and altogether unhealthier breed than Redman's. The typical rituals involved in human standoffs ensued between the two: there was some baring of teeth and a few growls, Redman making clear with his feet movements (which Jack was well placed to observe) on just whose territory the encounter was taking place. But, while there were no amiable markers like a handshake there were also no hostile barks, and after a few minutes, Redman seemed to have given the other man behaviouristic permission, and the entire party, to Jack's dismay and renewed sense of frustration at the short attention spans of humans in general, re-entered through the porch of 111 Maryland Lane. Jack led them into the front room, where he intended to remain, visible and sighing every so often, like a bad conscience, eyes judgmentally piercing whenever Redman looked at him, until the latter, with his obviously limited brain power, eventually remembered the training Jack had given him.

Redman, although he had admitted McNamara to his home, nonetheless found it difficult not to show that he was cross. "We couldn't do this in my office?" he said testily.

"Well," said McNamara, "I figured you might throw me out of there, you being so angry with me and all. And I thought if you wouldn't let me in or talk to me here, I could always put this safely through your letter box." He offered Redman a manila envelope.

"What's this?" Redman asked.

"It's a second USB drive with a copy of the data from the first one, plus a paper summary of the content of all one hundred and twenty-four calls, including a table of codenames used by Tweedledee and Tweedledum and my deciphering of them. In short, it's the stuff Miller gave you, with my glosses."

Redman emptied the contents on to his lap, and quoted McNamara to himself. "'As you can see, I have taken a hammer to it, James. You really don't want to get involved in this surreptitious business. I thought it best to remove the temptation.' So what's changed in a month, Robert?"

McNamara replied uncomfortably, "Remove the temptation from you, yes. I succumbed to it myself, obviously. And you have been justifiably angry with me. I am sorry for the deception. I hope I'm not rubbing salt into the wounds, but I thought that we might get over it if I gave it back to you and showed that it was not worth bothering about in the first place. You must have been wondering, I imagine. So that's what the summaries and codename table are for – as you can see, there's not a lot there to bother about. The call about Miller is of course scandalous, but nothing equals it, and that matter is officially closed. They do speak contemptuously and disrespectfully of members of staff but it's hardly the stuff of public disclosure."

Redman was studying the papers.

McNamara added, "I do apologise again for not giving you a choice. But I was concerned that you might be getting yourself into deep hot water."

"Thanks, dad," Redman replied. Then he looked up. "Your table of codenames pretty much tallies with mine, except I have a few more, and I haven't worked them all out. It took me a while to realise I was *Dr Watson*. But you haven't really answered my question, *Secretary of Defense*. Why did you change your mind?"

"Truly, genuine regret at the discord my action caused between us," said McNamara. "But what are you talking about, *your table of codenames*? How do you have a table of codenames? You gave me the impression you hadn't looked at the data."

Redman arose and stepped over the huffy, stewing Jack Russell. "Let's have some coffee," he said. "Then you can drive me into the office."

In the kitchen, over two cups of what McNamara found a stupendously bowel-moving brew dispensed from an expensive Italian coffee maker, Redman enlightened him thus: "I did not look at the data before you showed me the drive you destroyed. That's true. I was also incensed at what you had done. You removed my option. The deal was that you would keep the drive and I would sleep on the decision. In fact, I had on balance chosen to take your advice until the moment you told me you had decided for me by apparently shredding the data. Call me a contrarian, but from that point on I really wanted to have it. So, a few days later, when I took Miller's signed and finalised Compromise Agreement to his home, I asked him if he still had the recordings. He didn't. He had erased them. But he had something better – the original executable file. He went straight to a computer in his own house, logged on, installed the program on a random machine which runs twenty-four-seven in some University student computer room, and handed me the username and password for an untraceable email address. Whenever there's a call to or from Tweedledum or Tweedledee, an email gets sent to that address with a link I can go straight to and access the archived recording. The email server and the audio files are not even in the country – they're in North Korea or somewhere else that hasn't signed some treaty or other. It's apparently beyond all reasonable detection. So for the last few weeks, thanks to your patronising unilateral making up of my mind for me, I've had a live wiretap up on all their phone conversations."

McNamara felt a movement in his intestines like the shifting of tectonic plates. "I don't suppose I have any ground anymore to counsel against involving yourself in such a course of action. Can I at least ask what are the results?"

Redman made a puffing noise. "Mixed. Obviously when Covet is here in Odium the phone calls between him and Asterisk are reduced, on some days non-existent. I imagine any sensitive business they discuss in person when they can. But you do realise that what Miller gave me were *only* the conversations *between* the two? The program actually records *all* the phone conversations made to and from both their University mobiles and office landlines. It captures *everything*."

McNamara's eyes widened as his lower bowel expanded. "I am going to have to use your toilet in a minute, but tell me, how much data is that?"

"Well, predictably, dozens and dozens of calls a day. Frankly, I am just about drowning trying to keep up to date with it all and make sense of it. Phone discourse is so lacking in context, often broken, incoherent, miscellaneous. It refers all the time to other conversations or written information or a sphere of action the speakers have knowledge of but the eavesdropper doesn't. It mixes the trivial and the potentially momentous, but you regularly cannot distinguish one from the other. It's often like symbolist poetry, it seems to gesture penumbrally to things way beyond itself, and when you concentrate for any length of time on specific enigmatic utterances – in which if $x = y$ then the meaning is z but if $a = b$ the meaning must be c instead – you soon realise that simply by virtue of spending so much time on it you may be according it a significance which it possibly does not have. Then, if the same subject comes up again, which it can appear to, even in the very next phone call, you have to operate on the basis that either trivial meaning z or momentous meaning c may be under discussion, even though z or c are contradictory outcomes of a previous indeterminate reading. Thus numerous possible interpretations branch out exponentially. When you add to this the knowledge that these two guys deliberately use codenames, and possibly even codewords, at least with each other, but perhaps with others too, you get undecidability of enormous magnitude. In short, you can get lost pretty quickly in the maze of language and reference. But that's just about what they say. It's the meaning of pregnant silences which are truly difficult to crack: the import of things they don't say. It's a labyrinth, in a word."

"I have a bad feeling in my gut about all of this," said McNamara, "but thankfully that is a labyrinth whose contents more easily yield themselves up. Excuse me for a few minutes."

In Redman's upstairs toilet, a place McNamara, like most men, found congenial to brief meditation, he tried to meditate. Buddhists might think his seated absorption a lavatorial form of *zazen,* but on this occasion, failed Zen master that McNamara had never intended to be, it led not to the highest perfect awakening of *anuttarā-samyak-sambodhi,* nor the full enlightenment of *samyak-sambodhi,* or even the basic awakedness and understanding of mere *bodhi.* In fact, as McNamara noticed with gratification the pack of one hundred Coolwipes on Redman's bathroom shelf, he realised that his closeted thought processes had led him only into an old familiar kind of craving and desire he had tried so hard to abandon.

"I was not expecting this," he said to Redman after he came downstairs, "but can I make it all up to you by offering my assistance in the task?"

"I could do with some help," Redman replied.

In the front room, far out of earshot, forgotten by both of them, a sleeping dog lay.

Chapter Seven

25 October

"Here we are, Jane," said Buckrack, "two Americans abroad. Far from home. Thrown, inadvertently it seems, into one another's company. You're an east coaster and I'm a west coaster, but despite our differences we have more in common with each other than we do with our temporary hosts."

He left the seat he had taken opposite her and approached her in relaxed manner as he held forth.

"You ever seen dungeon porno, Jane? A lot of it starts like this, with a young, beautiful, shapely woman tied up, gagged, a hood over her head. I bet you have. Girls your age and of your type are always less innocent than they make out. You can imagine how it develops, the super-slow removal of the cloaking garments, the hood second last, of course, the duct tape round her mouth last, if at all, once the woman has been subdued and understands the need not to cry out, the obscene groping during the process which the girl is powerless to prevent, the probing of nether orifices with alien objects, her leisurely induction into unwilling submission." He approached until his lips were close to her ear. "Thing is, Jane, that's not what this is, and you're going to wish it was as trouble-free as that by the time I'm done."

He walked around the back of her. "You probably share my American puzzlement at the lack of basements in English houses, although in fact they're not so common in California. But then I discovered this loft space in this place they let me have, which in many ways is even better. It has these readily available beams I have cuffed you to, it's just as dark, if not darker, than any cellar, it's further from ground level, which makes it less likely any noise you make can be heard outside. It has only that one little skylight it's impossible to reach even if you could get free, and that one little trap door with an eight-foot drop you need ladders to negotiate without peril, even if you could unlock it from the inside, which you can't. And it's an empty house, I'm its only resident, and I'm new here, I have no friends yet, so no one visits. I'm sorry I had to keep you here all last night, but I had some errands to run, and I needed to make a point, and I confess I wanted you to be a little weary. It must have been cold too, no? What was that?"

Jane was writhing in her upright position and making humming noises of protest. She had been hoisted by a rope linked under the cuff chain that connected her wrists, so that her body was vertically elongated, her arms stretched high above her head until she stood virtually on tiptoe. Her ankles were also bound with rope. Buckrack took off the black hood. Jane blinked painfully in the harsh electric light from the single naked bulb, tears pricking her eyes. She had already been weeping. She was much more dishevelled in appearance than when she had turned the light on and first seen Buckrack in her apartment the night before. Her long hair was in disarray and her face marked by lines of despair. Once her vision had adjusted, she looked at him with wide, supplicating eyes, murmuring through the silver-grey heavy duty tape he had wound tightly round her mouth and the back of her head several times. She breathed heavily through her nose.

"Oh, I'll give you a chance to talk when I think the time is right, Jane. I'll even let you have some water. But for the next few minutes you need just to listen to me." He sat down again. "I realise that words only achieve so much, and I'm near the end of getting you to cooperate by means of merely verbal persuasion. I didn't need even much of that to take possession of item one, your passport." He lifted Jane's bag off the folding table next to his seat and removed the small booklet from it, showing it to her then throwing it on the table top. Next he extracted a blue purse. "Item two, your bank and credit cards and ready cash." Then a mobile telephone. "Item three. And, item four, the keys to your apartment." These he jingled before his face, smiling all the while, finally tossing them on the table with the other things. "And, finally, your iPad with, yes, oh dear, most of the relevant passwords, particularly to your email and Facebook accounts, saved by default, so that I don't even have to extort them out of you." This too he placed on the table surface.

"You wouldn't make much of a spy, Jane. Too incautious. These were all just sitting on your desk or in drawers in your apartment when I went in there last night to wait for you, apart from the keys, which I easily took from your hands as you stood there frozen in fear and amazement. And now that I have all these, Jane, I can exercise a considerable measure of control over your conduct when I set you free, which I assure you is what I intend, as long as you promise to behave yourself and do as you're told. Do we have a deal?"

Jane nodded vehemently.

"Clever girl," he said. "Are you thirsty?"

She nodded again.

"Anything to get that gag off, eh?" he mused. "I understand. In a moment."

He reached down to a supermarket bag at his feet and produced a long black woollen sock and a red-netted plastic box containing four medium-sized oranges. He ripped the net and placed the box on the table. Slowly, he took three of the oranges and dropped them one after the other into the open neck of the sock. Then he twisted the neck closed and twirled the fruit-filled sock around by flicking his right wrist.

"I don't know if this is true, but I once heard the claim on some TV show that oranges in a sock, used to beat someone, leave no visible bruises. What do you think, Jane?"

Jane's eyes narrowed and she shook her head, moaning feebly and twisting her body the little she could.

"Can't remember the name of the show," he said. "But it wasn't *Lost*, I can tell you that." Then he smiled at her knowingly. "*Lost*. I only started watching once I learned that you were studying it, Jane. I can't say I'm as big a fan as you seem to be, but tell me, is there anything from season one that the present situation reminds you of?"

Jane was still for a moment, then nodded her agreement.

"Yes, that's right. Sayid and Nadia. So touching. There he is, a committed torturer, tasked with getting information from and then executing a young woman much less, I must say, much less lovely than you, Jane. And he helps her escape instead, improbably, then falls in love with her, very unlikely, and spends all his time, because it is fantasticated TV after all, searching the globe for her, her photo in his pocket."

Jane looked at him fearfully.

"But that's not quite what's going to happen here, Jane. Oh, I am going to let you go. But I won't be showing you the same sentimental empathy. And why is that? Well, to begin with, I already have photographs of you, and I have already been searching for you, and it wasn't that difficult to find you."

Buckrack took one step towards her, swinging the sock through the air at his waist. It thumped on her left rib cage and her body swayed to one side as she let out a muffled shriek of pain.

"The second reason is that, as you remember, Nadia manages to convince Sayid, with little more than some shared banal nostalgia for their childhood and a ladylike palm caressing the back of his hand, that he is not *really* – whatever that means – a torturer. Personally, I find those flashbacks very sketchy and unconvincing in plot terms. It's a weak-minded viewer who doesn't acknowledge that the irony of Sayid being tortured by the mad ugly Frenchwoman in the present, on the island, has distracted us into craven gullibility about his past, that and the fact we are learning some petty new detail that has previously been withheld from us, namely who's the chick in the pic, the kind of titbit we sit before the screen for much of an hour, our right paw raised, waiting to be tossed."

He swivelled his body and hit her on the right side as if he were playing a backhand at tennis. She crumpled in the opposite direction, with a cry that seemed to sound from under water, kept from falling only by the bonds which secured her to the beam.

"Well, I too am not by habit a torturer. But you are not

going to persuade me to do anything other than what I am now doing. In fact, you are the one who has compelled me to this and a few other acts of moral inexcusability of late."

He struck her again on the left side, forehand, harder this time. And again on the right, backhand, even harder.

"I guess you might never have wanted to be a fat girl 'til now," Buckrack said. "A spare tyre might absorb some of that impact, no? Funny how everything depends on the circumstances. We might love being ourselves in one situation, but wish we were entirely someone else in another."

He put the sock down, reached into the supermarket bag and produced a plastic bottle of water. "Drink?" he suggested. "That might stop you playing dead."

Jane roused herself as he came towards her again. She looked at him with insipid affirmation. He reached up and placed the opened bottle on the horizontal beam behind her. Then he reached into his pocket. "Here, in my right hand, is a small pair of cosmetic scissors, with which I shall, carefully, and without harming a pore of your pretty cheek, cut through the tape. Here, in my left hand, as you might be able to sense, is a much heavier duty pair of scissors, which, if I tighten them a little – yeah, you feel that? – are at the moment acting like a nipple clamp calibrated a bit on the pinchy side. Now, when I remove the tape, you are going to remain silent unless spoken to unless you want your right nipple on the floor and a lot of blood staining that neat white blouse. There will certainly be no shouting or screaming. If there is, the gag goes back on and the nipple comes off. You got that? Once you've had your water we'll have a short conversation which, if it goes to plan, will also result in your body remaining consistently intact. Okay?"

Rigid with discomfort and fear, Jane nodded pitiably.

Buckrack cut through the tape carefully on the left side of her mouth and then, with care, without tugging at it, peeled it slowly off her skin until her lips were exposed. He left the flap of tape dangling. Jane was silent. He took the bottle and offered it to her. She drank slowly, their eyes meeting.

"I need," she said in a whisper, "to go to the bathroom."

He observed her calmly. "I understand," he said. "It's of no particular consequence to me if you do it in your pants, as I have a garden hose outside I can just reel in here and blast you with after making you strip down. But drink the rest of the water, then answer the couple of questions I have, and then you can go to the bathroom. As I say, if you can't wait, be my guest."

He held the bottle to her lips again and Jane gulped the water until it was empty.

"I repeat, Jane," said Buckrack, moving away and returning to his seat, "you're *so* incautious. I mean, that water could have had anything in it. Rohipnol, say, or something else to encourage you to acquiesce. But don't worry, it didn't. I think we already have an understanding, and before you leave here in a little while we shall have an even deeper compact that will ensure, if you value the skin on your back or the nipples on your front, that you do exactly as I say. That way you won't be punished again or worse. But I will come to that."

He picked up her iPad and opened the cover. "For now the one thing I need is the username of your bank account – the one "Daddy" pays into regularly – and your account password. If you hesitate to give me those, or you mess me around, like you pretend you don't remember them or give me the wrong ones, then I'll put the gag back on, let you shit or pee yourself, or both, then reel in my hose, get you naked, get you wetter but cleaner, and then some. I should explain why I want access to your bank account, in case you suspect I am a common thief. It simply makes it more easy for me to control what you do once I let you go, because without access to cash or credit, without a passport, without your email and Facebook accounts – oh, did I tell you I had changed the passwords on those already? – you are a little limited in your capabilities and correspondingly somewhat dependent on me. I only want this to be so for a short time, mind you. I have no wish to deprive you permanently, not of your liberty, certainly not of your charming bodily parts, not even of the money. So I am going to leave whatever I find in your account untouched. I am not here with the intention of confining you for long, or disfiguring you, or robbing you. But I am going to lock you out of your account for a little while. As long as you grant a few further requests, you will get out of this present situation before evening falls, with little more loss of joy than a few future nightmares. You will also stay out of prison. That is a promise."

Jane swallowed heavily. "Who are you?"

Buckrack sighed. "Actually, I intend to tell you that also before I let you go, because it will make all of this infinitely more comprehensible to you. But for the moment, and because you want to go to the bathroom, could you let me have the bank details, please?"

Somewhat timorously, she ventured, "If it *is* sex you want, there are easier ways."

Buckrack looked genuinely shocked. He shook his head. "Jane, Jane, Jane. A nice try at being Nadia, if a tad more sassy. But I agree. If it were sex I wanted, there are easier ways. You should therefore conclude, as I've already intimated, that sex is not what I want. Now please stop playing for time. All you'll do is soil yourself. The bank details? I can see from your card that it's www.bostonsixthbank.com, and I am on their site already."

Somewhat in a whimper, Jane said, "The username is all one word, 'songsofinnocence', no upper case."

Buckrack entered the details into the iPad keyboard and waited. "A reference to your poetic namesake, huh? That's cute. And the password?"

"It's 'songsofexperience'."

Buckrack chuckled. "Real cute, real cute. Now, it's asking me for the second, third and seventh characters of what it calls your 'gateway code'."

"All capitals. H, E, A".

"Just give me the whole thing, for my records."

"Capitals T-H-E, numeral 4, capitals Z-O-A-S."

"Is that one of Blake's too? A lesser known one?"

"Yes."

"Well, I'm going to change that, then I'm going to change the other two as well to things much more recondite that an *aficionado* of any one subject couldn't guess. Really, Jane, you make identity theft so easy. But hey, I'm in! Good girl. Okay, Jane, just under fifteen hundred a month, converted from sterling: a University of Odium research scholarship, I see? But a balance of over thirty thousand dollars, now how did that happen? Oh, look, another round two thousand dollars a month from Daddy too? And he really is called William Blake? Yet he doesn't pay you from his bank account but via a *PayPal account*? Then in May this two thousand suddenly becomes a one-off five thousand dollars, and then exactly two thousand a month again, until the first of this month, and suddenly another five thousand. A bit strange and irregular, no? No doubt you have an explanation, but don't even try me: I know more than you think. And it's a lot of money for a postgrad student." He looked at her and smiled. "I see that you've been making regular transactions, right up till yesterday, small sums too, supermarket stuff, Amazon. So this really is your main account, huh? Well, that's what I wanted. I don't see a card for any British account in your purse, and this account tallies with the American card you have, so I am going to assume this is all there is right now. I'll let you have some cash for necessities when I let you go. If by chance you have another source of funds I think you are going to be very careful about how you use it once we've had our closing chat. Now be silent while I lock you out of this particular account. The bathroom is only moments away, I promise. I hope you can contain yourself."

After a few minutes, he closed the iPad. "Done!" he reported amiably. "Okay, Jane, you remember last night I played you a recording of the conversation you had in the Senior Common Room with Professor McNamara?"

She nodded dully.

"You can therefore logically conclude that there was recording equipment in that room and that Professor McNamara let me install it there. If I can put it this way, Jane, there are people in the University who are cooperating with my enquiries. They may have needed some convincing as to why, and from a properly recognised authority, but that clearly happened, so they know more than they seem to. So you mustn't be too trusting of anyone once I let you go. It should be obvious that you've been under investigation for some time. So here are a few rules to this game of ours. If you like, I'm releasing you on a kind of parole, and I need surety of your compliant behaviour. Professor McNamara is under instruction to do and say nothing else in respect of these matters. If you say anything to him about the recording, or about what has happened between us, you can expect him to react with studied incomprehension, as if you are an idiot or a lunatic. He does not, in any case, know that I abducted you, tied you up and slapped you about a bit. I admit he would find that a bit unorthodox. But he has played his small part in this matter, and it is at an end. Therefore, as you will inevitably encounter him, you should behave as if none of this took place at all, and as if he knows nothing of it. If you don't then you can expect to fail this probationary test of mine, and to experience predictable consequences. One thing I shall certainly do is remove all that cash from your account, before I do other stuff that's even nastier and more permanent. Are we on the same page?"

Weak with pain and fear, Jane agreed.

"You can also conclude," Buckrack continued, "that there was a microphone in your apartment and that it's still there. That will be monitored continuously, and not just by me. As I've tried to make clear, you should assume I am not working alone. Now I know it will be your instinct, when I let you go back there, to try to find the microphone and dispose of it. But let me advise that you will almost certainly not find it, but that even if you do, you had better leave it where it is. I will know if you destroy it or move it, obviously, and that will only lead me to come round and visit some further punishment on you. Therefore why bother looking? Until further notice, if you wish to leave your apartment for any reason you will call me at a number I will give you and I will assess the reasons for your request and either grant or deny it. If I call you and you fail to pick up within ten rings, day or night, you can expect me or others at your door or on your tail pretty quickly. I am now also going to give you some detailed advice on how to conduct yourself in the next few days and weeks when you are not in your apartment, and particularly about the thorny and unexpected problem that you have created in respect of Dr Poon. But before I do that, I want to show you a photograph."

Buckrack reached into his shirt pocket and took out a regular six-by-four of a man around thirty years old and a woman of roughly the same age, who both held a small baby. The adults in the photo were smiling broadly.

When Jane saw the picture her already pale face visibly blanched.

Buckrack looked down, then up again. "Well, if that didn't make you shit your pants, Jane, maybe you're not so desperate after all."

Chapter Eight

25 October

That evening, as Jane was in fact released by Buckrack, and went stumbling back to Coolwipe Hall, stunned and panicked by the enormity of her kidnapping, Buckrack's violence and the now hostile stamp which every object in the world seemed to possess, McNamara was sitting with Redman in 111 Maryland Lane. He had returned, not so much to help Redman with the task of understanding Asterisk's and Covet's calls, but to persuade him that the wiretap was a lost and dangerous cause. He knew that things were too far gone for mere moral persuasion, so had decided that the best course was to demonstrate that the practical returns from such surveillance were seriously outweighed by the risks in carrying it on. He was aware, while he listened to all the calls with Redman, that this approach created a risk of its own: Redman might think that he was permanently joining forces with him in his shady endeavour. But he felt confident that the exercise would demonstrate the truth without explicit exhortation. In this he was to prove quite mistaken.

"The problem is, James," he said as they sat drinking scotch afterwards, "you're going about it in the wrong way. I don't know what it is about postmodern literary people like you, but you are far too preoccupied with what you don't understand, with the slipperiness of meaning, than with what is so obviously graspable. These are phone calls made with generally practical purposes in mind, conducted on the hoof, not tissues of carefully crafted language, texts to be explicated. Most of the gaps in your understanding are caused by simple lack of context. Any call can refer to some other piece of information you don't have, or decision you don't know about, and so its full import evades you. What's your instinct? To worry over its meaning, to promote that worry into a paranoiac suspicion that if you could crack its code then you would have access to some startling, scandalous truth? There are so many calls like that, and the task of interpreting them would be endless. I say the best thing is to ignore all that. Pay no attention especially to the tatty, unprofessional way in which they talk about the staff, the insulting *noms de plume*, and so on. Focus on what you want to know, and don't be distracted by what you happen to find. I assume what you want to know is anything affecting the Union or its negotiations with management. Well, what have you found? Not much."

"Granted," Redman replied. "But I don't agree. For example, there's the call Asterisk had with Poon about the management proposal to link Annual Performance Review with salary increments. So, we have him calling Covet prior to that and Covet telling him that if the Union holds out against the proposal he should concede and they will try again in a year. But Covet tells him to try horse trading with a handful of minor morsels, things the Union has wanted for a long time, especially time off for the President for Union activities, and additional payment for Union officers invited onto union-management working groups. Asterisk then calls Poon immediately after, before the Union meeting which was planned to discuss the proposal, and he tells her that, although management has a legal duty to consult with the Union about the proposal, it is going to enforce it anyway, whatever the Union thinks. We know from his call with Covet that this is a lie: if the Union stands firm in its opposition, he's been instructed to back down. But he throws her the morsels he has been told to, which happen to include a personally tasty piece for her as President. He's even got this costed and presents it as a thirty-plus-thousand-pounds *per annum* subsidy that management is giving to the Union, even though they have a legal obligation to allow officers time off or payment *in lieu* for Union activities which they have simply never honoured. There's no mention that the proposal will save the University over a quarter of a million on the annual wage bill as well as put our members under the cosh of performance-related pay. Poon swallows this lie whole, no doubt because of the big sugared pill she personally sees it as. She then comes to the meeting – I was there – and informs us that management are going to enforce the proposal. She tells us nothing about the phone call with Asterisk. Instead, *she* argues that we should not resist the proposal but go back to management and bargain to the Union's advantage in return for our agreement. The net result is that the Union executive agrees, although I didn't personally, Poon goes off to Asterisk, gets what he's already offered her, and some individuals on the Union executive come out of it better off, her most of all, while the membership as a whole comes out of it very badly. The entire thing is perverse. All that seems to me pretty important to know."

McNamara had listened patiently. "But what's your

point? So what, Covet and Asterisk outplayed Poon at poker. That's how the union-management game gets conducted up and down the land. They bluffed and won this hand. It's frustrating, perhaps, but hardly surprising. There's no point getting vexed when you find out your opponent had weaker cards than you thought. And it's exactly what you did to Asterisk in the Miller case. You beat him at poker."

"I beat him because I had a fucking royal flush, not because I bluffed!" Redman exclaimed. "And I had that hand because Miller was deliberately dealing me great cards. I'm not bemoaning the loss of this hand. I'm saying that if we can see what cards Asterisk and Covet have we can't be so easily bluffed. And this simple little computer program lets us see their cards."

"It lets *you* see their cards," McNamara corrected. "But it's hard to play poker with a big mirror behind your opponent and get away with it. Sooner or later they may look over their shoulder and figure out how you're doing it."

"It's a bad analogy, Robert. First of all, it's not a big mirror behind them they can just turn round and see. It's more like I'm telepathic. It's a tiny piece of code on an anonymous University workstation that sends recordings of their conversations to some godforsaken lawless outback, from where I anonymously retrieve them using an untraceable email address. Even if they discovered it, that's not going to lead them to me."

"In which case, what will draw attention to you will be the pre-emptive actions you may take based on information you gain by underhand means. And you do know this is criminal. What are you taking such a risk for?"

"Oh, listen to yourself, Robert. Covet and Asterisk have

done criminal things under the radar for years, you and I both know it. Now when I employ the same methods you wax lyrical about the wrong."

"It's not about the wrong. It's about the risk. It's also about what it will do to you, how it will distract you, how it threatens to consume you, how it will perhaps damage you, never mind the fact that it may ruin you. Look at what it's done already: you suspect Poon of being corrupt, or at least weak-willed, so now you will be on the lookout for other such instances, on guard against her."

Redman scoffed. "*You* are going to lecture *me* about being suspicious of *Poon*? You've never trusted her."

"But I'm not acting on my mistrust. That's the difference. I've removed myself from any position where my mistrust of her has any relevance."

"Ah," Redman said. "Perhaps we should talk about that, Robert. You removing yourself from a position. Because it's what you have also wanted me to do for a long time, and I have never figured out why. I mean, like everybody else, I've never known why you resigned in the first place, much less why you think I should follow suit."

"I resigned for an obvious reason. It was doing me no good."

"It wasn't a position to be pursued for the benefits to yourself. There was a greater good you were meant to be pursuing."

McNamara grunted with indignation and seemed about to give vent to his feeling, but then he checked himself. "You know I know that, and you know that I did pursue that. I think it's obvious what I am saying, because you just gave an example of it yourself. We might as a Union have wished to pursue a greater good, but most of the time as officers we were frustrated from doing so, or at best put a finger in the dyke until the flood returned to wipe us out a year later. I did the work for nine years, James. I hardly gave up at the first discouragement. But after that period, when I did an accounting of my effort compared to the benefits, all I could truly point to were a half a dozen personal cases in which I had made a serious difference to individuals: an early retirement on health grounds here, an over-the-top disciplinary case there. Maybe I was not personally very effective, but no one else seemed to want to do it. Even Poon, as far as I understand it, had virtually to be press-ganged into it after I resigned. You might well condemn her compromises and subterfuges. But all the causes I would have considered worth making a principled stand for at the beginning of my period had been lost by the end of it, and not for lack of trying on the Union executive side. And I was a lot more experienced than Poon as far as politics goes, and I still carry pretty serious ideological baggage. But the problem is, I decided, that it's not really a Union at all, but a professional association, with a membership that is largely atomised and individualistic. The members are essentially greedy, self-centred, competitive careerists of the most stab-you-in-the-back kind, hardly heroes of solidarity. Academics are, on the whole, with a few exceptions, despicable human beings, driven by craven self-interest. The members to this day include a Dean of Faculty, Blandford, who tweets people every time he is cited in a journal, who is so stupid that he thinks an absence of real intellectual gravitas can be compensated for by advertised self-importance, which has developed into a real psychosis in which he thinks that Twitter has made him a public figure, and that anything he tweets, from having a cup of tea in the morning to getting extra booths in a toilet, is *de facto* noteworthy. But things can get worse than having members who happen to be idiots in high places. Even Pro-Vice Chancellors, sitting on the other side of the table from us at pay talks, were sometimes members. What kind of union permits its members to act expressly with the interests of management in mind in union-management negotiations or voting situations? Damn it, even Asterisk qualifies for membership, and you couldn't deny him it if he applied. But then, the rank-and-file, as it used to be called, is torpid and inactive. We had difficulty getting quorate ordinary meetings unless the issue of parking spaces was on the agenda. In fact, back then, it *was* the *Association of University Teachers*, too timid even in name to wish to be tarred with the brush of being a trades union. It's only recently started calling itself the University and College Union, and that only after a merger."

Redman leaned over to top up McNamara's glass. He retorted, "In what way does any of that argue against what I am doing? All it amounts to saying is that conventional, time-honoured methods are bound to fail. I am proposing a departure from such methods. I am suggesting that the only way to make a difference is by adopting nefarious tactics similar to those deployed by Tweedledum and Tweedledee."

McNamara sighed. "Make a difference? Oh, the romance of it all! Have you noticed how much the language of the left tempts us into feeling that we can do something finite that will make a permanent change? But this is not an epoch of revolution, James. It won't bring forth an outlaw like Trotsky who can engineer a gear shift so profound, even on a small scale, that the vehicle can never again be thrown into reverse. And even if you could, at what cost to yourself? Before you dismiss what I'm saying, I don't just mean legal *risk*. I mean at what cost to yourself, to your being? Really, what impulse is being followed here, what is the determining aim of the access you now have to these private conversations? Was Miller looking for justice or revenge?"

"He expressed an interest in 'nailing' them. I guess it was either, or both."

"And you? Do you want to 'nail' them as well?"

"I want to outwit them. I know I'm finished negotiating with them, because they never have real negotiations anyway. When they can't use *force majeure*, they constantly try to move the goalposts, or if that fails they resort to strategies which are little short of corrupt or even illegal, and if they are found out in those attempts they pretty much use outright bribery. So I guess I feel it's time to fight fire with fire, and all Miller did was give me the means."

"But why not just walk away and do what you came to work in a university for?"

"Maybe, for one thing, because I am forty, not sixty, Robert. I have twenty-five plus years to go on surviving in an institution like this, whereas you could probably retire tomorrow if you had to. There is also the fight-the-good fight argument and to hell with whether you win or lose. Not to mention the fact that I wouldn't be surprised if I did manage to turn up some public scandal worth blowing the whistle on, given what I already know about Covet and Asterisk and how they operate. So I have reasons not to buy into your quietism. I'd rather not retreat into the study right now and write my own defeatism up. Look what happened to you."

McNamara was stultified in a near-muted way. "What do you mean?"

"Well, shortly after you resigned, off you went and wrote a book with the worst title in the world: *Actually Non-Existing Communism*. Curious, that at just that point you should write not a rallying cry to a new socialist politics, but an account of the God that failed."

"Oh, for Christ's sake, James, I'm a political scientist, not a manifesto writer. The book was about the substantial difference between Marx's conceptions of communism and what happened in the USSR, China, Cuba, *etcetera*. I think it said some things that still needed to be said, with some detailed contemporary case studies, namely about Marx's conception that co-mmunism would only take off in advanced capitalist countries, not the backward feudal ones that laid claim to it, and about the serious intellectual mistakes we make if we equate Marxism with what actually occurred under the name of 'real socialist' revolutions. I don't see what was defeatist about it."

"No, but it's how it was manipulated, the arguments it was used to support. Did you notice that every popular review basically made out that it supported the thesis that socialism had proved to be a dead-end, and Marxism therefore an historical aberration?"

"Yes, but the academic reviews didn't say that."

"Who reads them? And the TV interviews? That Discovery Channel history of the post-Cold War you appeared on, for example? You might as well have been Francis Fukuyama. Its general thesis was that liberal capitalism was the best we could hope for."

"I can't control how selectively I am read or edited. I know the book did not say that, and anyone who really reads it knows that. The book's the thing, not coverage of it. What I argue and what the media present me as arguing are not the same. And in the end, whatever misconceptions others have, in myself I am content with what I did."

"My point," Redman went on forcefully, "is precisely

that you don't control these things, and you're being naïve if you think the book itself, however well it's done, with its relatively small readership, has the same influence as those accounts of it. That's why you shouldn't be content. Sure, this is what the liberal media do with a book like yours: they process it according to some familiar ideological template. Just as I can't control Poon or Asterisk the ways things are. So I'll break the rules instead. I won't observe the template, because observing the template means we lose nearly all the time, or can hope for stalemate on a few select issues at best."

"*My point*," McNamara said, "is that it was *academic* work *about* politics and economics. It was an attempt to get people to think straight about a complex issue. It was not a *political* work that aimed to get people to act in a cause. I could argue with you that getting our thinking straight might *lead to* more rational actions but I'm not even bothered to justify it that way. It needs no such justification. I was doing what an academic is meant to do."

"And *my further point* is that right now I am not interested in doing what academics are meant to do when Tweedledum and Tweedledee are corrupting the very institution in which they are meant to do it. If they get their way academics a generation younger than you won't get to do what they are meant to do, you see? Damn it, we might already be at that stage, for all we know. And if we are, then me turning aside to finish – ah, who am I kidding? to start! – my bloody book on Raymond Williams is just folly. This way at least I get to find out what exactly it is they are doing. And it just happens to be me in this position. No one else is. So yes, as I said before, someone has to do it, and that someone, yes, in the present situation, has to be me. You can help, which would be welcome, or at least not hinder, which is pretty much all you have done."

They were silent for some time. Redman tilted his glass to suggest a refill. McNamara was thoughtful. "I am not intending to help you further with this beyond this evening," he said decisively. "But I will pitch in with my thoughts on what we have listened to, as we've already come that far. And of course I will say nothing to anyone about it."

Redman poured from the bottle dejectedly. "Okay. Well, then, as we seem to have settled that, I'm listening."

McNamara sipped. "I repeat, so far there isn't much that's Union-related, although I can accept the obvious point that there probably will be. I also repeat, focus on what you *can* understand without too much inter- pretative work: that might help you with what you don't get. It's tempting to think that things are in code when they are just discreetly expressed. The one thing we know is coded are the names of a number of members of staff, but we were able to work all of those out virtually independently. Your list and mine are the same."

Redman took up a piece of paper from the table between them. "All except one," he said. "*Avenger* does not appear in any of the calls Miller recorded and so isn't on your list. Yet it appears on numerous occasions in the ones I've eavesdropped on. I can't work out who it refers to. But it strikes me as one hell of a code name."

McNamara shrugged. "Perhaps we should listen to those calls again," he answered wearily.

PART THREE
26 OCTOBER – 29 OCTOBER

Chapter Nine

26 October – 27 October

If it is in their thirties that men truly become aware that they are not indestructible, and in their forties that they generally experience the first serious twinges of mortality and loss of life force, then it is in their fifties that they begin to see signs of their future end on the horizon. In the case of Professor Sir Evan Covet, aged fifty-seven at the time of this narrative, this was so.

It had begun one morning ten years before when he awoke with a mysterious pain to the left of his solar plexus. At first he thought it might be a cracked rib or simply some muscular strain, but as months passed and the ache persisted without diminishing, he began to worry that it might be something more hostile. The area was not far from the heart, and when he looked up diagrams of that organ he considered the inferior vena cava the only passageway so positioned as to be the likely source of the problem. His fantasies of some impending aneurysm or possible sudden thrombosis (both things he had not at first fully understood but after meticulous research came to know the full intricacies of) were allayed by his private doctors, who pointed out that the posterior vena cava, as it is also called, derives its name from the fact that it enters the rear of the heart, carrying blood up alongside the spine from the abdominal region. It could not be the cause of a pain in the front of the body. For the same reason, his occasional nightmares of cancer of the spleen, which he knew could kill a person in weeks, were dismissed. They were also fairly sure it was not a problem with the lower oesophagal sphincter. After various tests, X-rays and a mid-body MRI scan, the doctors' best and vague guess was a "musculo-skeletal dysfunction" which was undetectable and probably nothing to worry overmuch about: just one of those things we can expect as we age, but unlikely to be debilitating or fatal. This had proved seemingly true over the years, but the problem remained chronic to this day, reminding him constantly that a small zone of his body was dully and recalcitrantly refusing to do its job efficiently and in cooperation with the rest. It was not the kind of thing that painkillers could combat. Infrequently there were small sharp needling pains in the area which felt like they were occurring just under the surface of the skin. If he made any abrupt upper body turns to the right the region tightened into a knot of inhibiting, though not excruciating, pain. But it was worst when he coughed or laughed. Either activity stimulated the muscles in the area to convulse, and with each contraction and expansion he experienced something like a stabbing sensation, which often sent his right hand groping towards it in alarm. He therefore trained himself to avoid situations in which he might cough or laugh much.

Two years or so after the unilluminating diagnosis, he woke up in the middle of the night in a five star Cape Town hotel (it is odd how often these things emerge during sleep: you can go to bed feeling perfectly fit but be aroused in a state of horrible mortal fear) because he had a throbbing in his left hip. He put his hand down there and could actually feel the muscles spasming and rippling. He had an ominous sense of something very bad about to happen, when what felt like a crack of lightning struck from the hip to the knee, as if a whip had been lashed inside his leg. He started up bodily and howled, or rather emitted a sound which was like a loud low moan and a high pitched squeal combined. He managed to get himself upright before the next attack came, and when it did it sent him crashing naked to the floor, gibbering in severe distress and, because it was so entirely unexpected, serious fear. He was too terrified and preoccupied by the shock to be able to formulate words. All that came out of him were unrepressed small shrieks and heaving sighs. His conduct so frightened the mediocre black prostitute who was with him that, instead of using the bedside phone at which he gestured to call for help, she hurriedly threw on her clothes and made a swift escape from the room, leaving him clutching his thigh with both hands and rocking his body on the carpet. The recurring pulses, burning, stinging like electricity with some excess voltage pangs added for good measure, did not stop for ten minutes, by which time he was in real tears, for the first time he could remember, certainly the first time since childhood. The attacks came again the next day while he was trying to relax in the jacuzzi, and his reaction half flooded the hotel bathroom. He checked himself into a private hospital nearby, where a far from mediocre white consultant instantly diagnosed sciatica, and told him, incredibly, "not to worry" because he had not slipped a disc.

"It first happened to me," the doctor said, "though in the other leg, when I was thirty-eight, so you can count yourself lucky at your age."

Covet wanted to know if it was likely to occur again.

"Maybe," the doctor replied.

"Did it happen again to you?" Covet asked.

"Sure," nodded the doctor laconically.

"What can I do to prevent it?"

"Well," said the doctor, perhaps with a certain sense of liberty from constraint because he was unlikely to see the patient again, "they say posture control, exercise, and stretching help. But I do all that and I still get it every so often. I recommend stoicism. It's the best medicine known to human kind."

And return it did, in the same leg, every two or three years. After the second episode, which occurred while he was driving his Mercedes on a rare family holiday and almost caused him to kill his wife and two teenage children as well as himself, Covet started to think there was something physically wrong with the left side of his body. More doctors told him there was little chance that the permanent crisis in his midriff was at all associated with the occasional attempted *coup d'état* in his sciatic nerve. But he could not help but think that the left wing nature of both was part of some constitutional eruption, perhaps even a sea change in the *zeitgeist* of his very brain. A CT scan of the latter revealed no relevant change in the structure of that organ. It was still pretty much the same thing that had got him his First Class Honours in Law from the University of Dundee. Nonetheless, his right side began to watch out for his left side as if it were some ailing Siamese twin. What his gold standard health package could not get him without personal cost – and it got him regular acupuncture, osteopathy, physiotherapy, angio-grams, biopsies, urinalysis, sigmoidoscopy, and a gamut of other miscellaneous tests and procedures and treatments – he invested in: posture chairs, back braces, a car with no clutch, memory cushions, Scholl foot arch supports, regular swims, an infrared sauna, to name but a few.

Yet still the waves kept coming in Canute's direction. On the day of his divorce, as he finally and reluctantly removed his wedding ring, he noticed that his left hand trembled while his right remained still. His dental issues appeared to occur only on the left side of his mouth, as did his tongue ulcers. He had a bout of psoriasis on the left elbow, and a fungal infection on his inner left thigh which, upon investigation, drew his attention to what was adjacent: a retracted left testicle, significantly higher than his right. His left eyelid, by contrast, was the one which drooped a little lower. When he looked at himself naked in the mirror, as he often now did, he thought he saw a curious asymmetry in his limbs and curves. He even took a high resolution digital photograph of his nude self against a black backdrop, divided it vertically in half, and examined the contrasting halves mathematically insofar as Adobe Photoshop and his insecure knowledge of geometry would permit. The exercise did not reassure him.

And then, eventually, one evening, as he sat in front of his fifty-two inch LCD home cinema watching the last episode of the first season of *Breaking Bad*, which he had consumed in back-to-back fashion over four evenings at his minor mansion, alone, mainly in darkness and rural autumnal silence, all through which he had felt his mind slowly whirring and speeding up to the velocity required for an incipient realisation, a kind of epiphany in slow motion, he arrived at a conclusion which, while astonishing, he felt intuitively to be correct. His ailments were a punishment. They had been visited upon him as retribution for an adult life which, he knew, had in almost every regard lacked virtue. It was not that he thought there was anything divine or demonic actually at work within him. While he had been raised in the Reformed Presbyterian Church of Scotland, and was to every external witness of his public conduct a Calvinist to the very marrow of his being, he knew himself to be, privately and in truth, a quite Godless man. He did not believe in any metaphysical actuality in which everyone is born a sinner, and as such is subject to God's wrath and the punishment of death, which means eternal separation from God in Hell unless the sinner repents and turns in faith to accept Jesus Christ as the only means of salvation. The only part of this ridiculous proposition he subscribed to was that everyone is born a sinner, which was exactly why, he reflected, he had thoroughly revelled in duplicity, vice and hatred from the day of his first full academic appointment in Edinburgh: it was the natural state of Man and not something to be considered unusual, just something you should try to be better at than others.

But the developing story of Walter White, as he watched it fascinatedly, reached out to him over four nights some spiritual tentacle which seemed to proffer an hitherto untouched insight into his ongoing physical malaise. Walter, upon being diagnosed with cancer, could be seen descending abjectly from loving husband, father and dutiful Chemistry schoolteacher into crystal meth dealer, liar and murderer, in a way that could not conceivably end well for him at the far-off conclusion of season five. As Walter's physical integrity began to collapse, so too did his moral sense at the same rate abandon him. It hardly took a major leap of logic (or newly found spiritual wisdom) on Covet's part to understand that an ethical regeneration might also restore his own corporeal balance. The trick, he realised, was to be Walter White in reverse: to live Walter's life backwards, away from wickedness in the direction of the good.

Covet retired to bed, feeling peculiarly light-headed, although he had drunk no Drambuie, as was his regular evening habit. He experienced some sleepless hours, but not as an insomniac does, writhing in frustration at his failure to appease Morpheus. Rather, he conned and cast up to himself his lifetime of deceit and infidelity, his many backstairs manoeuvrings and masterful man-ipulations, his bullying, his loathing, his prejudices and superiority, his consuming avarice and addictive double dealing, his confidence tricks, his glorious blackmail gambits and mind-game victories. This was done not in a spirit of remorse, but as if they were so many sandbags he was now capable of throwing out of his rapidly ascending balloon: *ad astra*, as it were, but not *per ardua*. He was priest to his own confessor, forgiving himself without need of either benediction or penance. At last he fell into a peaceful sleep, and dreamed, joyfully, that he was Adam, alone in the Garden of Eden.

The dream ended with the sound of hammering. It took him some moments to realise that someone was banging heavily at his front door, many metres away downstairs. This was unusual: Homestead Park was no Eden, but it did have twenty-four hour perimeter security, and un-announced visitors were a virtual impossibility. He thought it must be his chauffeur, and that he had overslept, but when he looked at the clock he saw that it was not yet 6am. He got out of bed, put on a dressing gown and nimbly walked the long walk along the upstairs hallway, the rapping at the door increasing in volume but not yet having for him, as it might have by now for the reader, any suggestions of *Macbeth*, the primrose way or the everlasting bonfire. As he started to descend the staircase, indeed, he remarked on his sobriety and the fact that, despite his foreshortened sleep, he felt curiously alert and, well, *well*. Crossing the large drawing room to the front lobby, he strode across the vestibule and approached the outer door.

Parting the curtain, he saw the glaring face of Buckrack, and reacted with an internal alarm he only just managed to conceal.

"Open up," Buckrack said through the glass.

Covet unlocked the door and hissed, "What the hell?"

Buckrack pushed past him and he closed the door and locked it once more. He pursued Buckrack into the drawing room, where he found him standing beside a coffee table.

"How on earth did you get here?" Covet demanded. "How do you know where I live?"

Buckrack made a sound of exasperated disbelief. "You're surprised at *that*? I am ex-CIA, remember. These things are pretty easy to me."

"But how did you get past security?"

Buckrack winced in amusement. "British country residential park security? I may be sixty-two but you think I can't scale a wall and avoid cameras?"

"But we *agreed*," said Covet forcefully. "No personal contact. You're meant to use the mobile number I gave you."

"Yeah, well, something came up. No one is gonna know I came here, but I wanted to get you before you went in to work."

Covet eyed him with anxiety. "What do you mean?"

"I need some coffee," Buckrack said.

"You need coffee?" Covet repeated impatiently.

"Yeah, the news will keep."

"Christ!" Covet exclaimed, and turned towards the kitchen. Buckrack removed his coat and threw it on a sofa, then planted himself beside it.

Five minutes later, Covet was holding a breakfast mug in his hands and watching Buckrack remove a photo from his bag, printed on plain white copy paper.

"Do you know this girl?" Buckrack asked him. "Ever met her before?"

Covet picked up the photo and examined it. "No. Not that I can remember, at any rate. Who is she? And why?"

"Her name is Jane Blake. She's a postgraduate student at Odium."

"I know hardly any students. I meet them occasionally for photo opportunities, but mostly I avoid them."

"She's a beautiful girl. You'd remember her if you'd met her, right?"

"Not my type," Covet rejoined.

Buckrack laughed. "I think she's one of those girls who's pretty much any man's type. Maybe even any woman's type. She's sex on legs through any set of eyes. She's in the Department of Cultural Studies. Her supervisor is Poon."

Covet tried to look more interested. "I see. So?"

"She's also a pastoral tutor in McNamara's student residence. Does that ring any bells?"

Covet appeared faintly enlightened. "Ah," he said. "I am beginning to remember now. Yes, I asked McNamara to give her that role. She needed a place to stay. He was a bit reluctant to bypass the usual selection process, but he gave in. It's coming back to me. But I don't remember her being in Cultural Studies. I thought she was in the School of English."

"Why did you do that?"

119

"Why did I do what?"

"Why did you make a special effort to find a postgrad student somewhere to live? Don't you have an accommodation office for that? A bit beneath your level, no?"

"Normally I wouldn't concern myself with that kind of thing, but she was one of the students who got a Vice Chancellor's Research Scholarship. I sometimes help these students out, as my office is attached to their award, and there are very few of them. Yes, I remember now. That's how I might have met her. But that was nearly a year ago. And my memory may be defective, but I'm sure she wasn't in Cultural Studies. Anyway, stop beating about the bush. Why are you asking?"

Buckrack raised his hand. "In a moment," he said. "She *was* on the English programme, but at the beginning of this academic year she transferred into Cultural Studies. Change of direction in her Ph.D., apparently. But this Vice Chancellor's scholarship, who makes the decision on that?"

Covet sighed. "It's open to nominations from across the University. If you are a Head of School you can apply on behalf of any new postgraduate research student. I chair a small committee which looks at the nominations, I take their advice, and then I make the final decision. That's why it's called the Vice Chancellor's Research Scholarship: it's in my gift. I only ever normally meet the students when they arrive and take up their award, and even then it's usually just a five minute handshake job for a feature in the University *Newsletter*."

Buckrack put down his coffee and looked levelly across the table. "It seems a little weird to me that you hire me to monitor Poon and McNamara, the current President and the previous President of the Union, and here we have someone else with relatively regular one-to-one access to both of them, partly because of your efforts. I have bugged their offices, and she is often in both of their offices. Now, I thought what you wanted was inside information on the Union's activities. I didn't think conversations with students were likely to be interesting. But what I'm beginning to wonder is whether one of the things you actually want me to hear and report on is what she discusses with them?"

Covet smiled in the negative. "This is what I'm paying you for? You're way off. For a start, I hardly know this girl. The only thing I ever did was put her in McNamara's Hall. I didn't know she was going to end up being supervised by Poon. It's just a coincidence. And I agree with you. I can't see how what she discusses with them can conceivably be of any interest to us."

"But why McNamara's Hall? Why ask a guy you have very poor relations with? Why not lean on someone else, another Warden likely to be more unquestioningly obedient?"

"Okay," Covet shrugged, "I did it to irritate him. I knew he would protest about normal procedure, equal opportunities, that kind of thing, and I wanted to take some pleasure in reminding him who was boss. I didn't get much. He caved in pretty quickly."

"A coincidence, then," Buckrack echoed. "Well, it's turned into a pretty interesting coincidence. That's why I'm here."

Covet patiently clasped his hands under his chin. "Go on," he encouraged.

"Okay," said Buckrack. "As you know, I currently have three microphones up and running: one in McNamara's study in Coolwipe Hall, and one each in Poon's office and Redman's office in the Trump Building. They are high spec omnidirectional mics and they record in pretty good quality any sound or speech in the room, even at the furthest spatial extremes from the mic. That's why they were fairly expensive. They are noise activated and send a wireless audio signal after activation to a receiver in my house, to which recording equipment is attached. I can even record conversations happening simultaneously in any of the three rooms. The results so far have been what I have given you: not a lot, pretty much standard Union business in Poon's office, the odd phone call about Union business in Redman's office, and nothing at all in McNamara's study. Until the night before last, that is."

Covet opened his palms. "And what happened the night before last?"

"Listen for yourself," said Buckrack. "I came out here to let you hear this."

He placed a recorder on the table and played the discussion between McNamara and Jane Blake.

When it was over, Covet said, "It's not without interest. McNamara gave her reasonable advice. I think everyone knows Poon is gay, no news there. All it is, though, is she's doing the dirty deed with this girl and there's an undeclared conflict of interest. There's not a lot I can do with that, however."

"Not on its own," Buckrack agreed. "But now we know. It won't be difficult to get evidence in a form you can use. It's just a matter of setting it up, and I wanted to know if you'd like me to do that. I'm sure you can force her resignation or fire her based on that and, pretty much at a stroke, you've sabotaged the Union. That's the kind of thing you've been after, no?"

"Well, yes," Covet acknowledged in a judicious tone, "but she'd only be replaced by Redman. It's true that I wouldn't mind breaking them, but this wouldn't do it, it would only get rid of her. And in some ways Redman would be a bigger problem than she is as President. I was really more interested in finding out what they are planning and how they are responding to management proposals and initiatives. We've got a busy year of radical stuff ahead and I need to be able to stitch them up. We can keep this in our back pocket for now."

"So you don't want me to follow it up? This opportunity may not last. You heard yourself, the girl is trying to break it up."

"No," Covet said decisively. "I don't want this thing going too far afield, so we need to keep the student out of it, for now anyway."

"But I'll report any further conversations she has with McNamara or Poon?"

"Yes, do that."

At the door, Covet said, "You mustn't just arrive here like this again, no matter what comes up. Phone me on my personal mobile. We'll meet somewhere more out of the way if the need arises."

"Okay," said Buckrack.

"But there is one thing. Why did it take you two nights to tell me about this?"

"I didn't get to the recording 'til early this morning. I had been reviewing the others from Poon's and Redman's offices. Nearly all of it turned out to be dross, but nothing of any interest to us ever seems to occur in McNamara's study, so I tend to leave that stuff 'til last. I almost didn't listen to it at all when I realised she was just a student. But when I did I came over as soon as I could."

"Right," said Covet. "Thanks."

Covet shaved and showered. The encounter with Buckrack had come like a bitter aftertaste of everything bad he had been reckoning over in bed the night before, but he realised that it was unrealistic to expect that he could instantly follow his new path of virtue without clearing away the practical obstacles the past inevitably would leave in his way. In any case there was not much to tidy up. He would simply not pursue the matter of Poon and her new paramour. He would wind Buckrack's surveillance operation down by telling him to discontinue it in a day or two. There would be no need to give Buckrack a reason: he would hardly complain if he was allowed to run out the remainder of his one-year contract in salaried idleness. He would even let him return to LA if he wanted, and never the twain should meet again. As he dried himself off he remarked that his body felt firmer and suppler than usual, and when he looked in the mirror he appeared less anxious and haggard than he often did. He also felt younger, lighter limbed. There was very little troubling his mind. In fact what dominated it was a sense of relief, akin to that experienced when you have been at some brink beyond which there is an abyss of danger or the unknown, and you draw back and purposefully walk away. It was a good feeling, a safe feeling, and one he could not remember ever feeling before. Perhaps he had been living close to that gulf for a lot longer than he imagined?

He even decided to make himself some scrambled eggs while he waited for his driver to arrive. This was a new thing too, as he normally had breakfast meetings in his private dining room at the University, and hardly ever cooked. Stirring the wooden spoon in the saucepan, hearing it thud hollowly against the edges, with the light dairy smell wafting up into his face, gave him a sense of domesticity and comfort. Instead of more coffee he made himself warm milk, which he had not drunk since he was a small boy, and wondered at its neutral, calming, unstimulating effect. He heard the car draw up at 7.30, just as he was finishing it. He took his briefcase and coat and exited the house.

It was still dark, though the sky was lightening prettily and the driveway was illuminated by the portico lamps. His driver, Brian Blackfoot, got out of the car at the bottom of the entry steps. He was a large portly man with a kind face and a thick avuncular moustache. But Covet noticed something in his greeting and his expression that lacked the usual geniality. He was about to ask if anything was wrong when he saw the rear doors open, and out stepped two men even larger than the chauffeur. He recognised them as Harmwell and Wolfitt, the Chief of University Security and his Deputy. They were wearing their customary black *Reservoir Dogs* suits and white shirts whose chilling effect Covet had often approved of, but which he did not relish now. Harmwell was holding a large buff envelope. His expression seemed a combination of pain, awkwardness, and determination. There seemed nothing promising in any of the three.

"Vice Chancellor," Harmwell nodded, but did not wait to be invited to start ascending the steps, followed by Wolfitt. As they approached Covet saw Blackfoot turn with resignation and get back into the driver's seat and close the door. In an instant the two security men were towering in front of him, their blackness and broad shoulders actually blotting out nearly everything he could catch of the morning sky.

"I am sorry about the unannounced visit, Vice Chancellor," said Harmwell, "but we are under instructions from the President of University Council. You are not to go into work today. I am told the letter in this envelope explains everything."

Covet felt feeble. These men normally did his peremptory bidding without question, but there was a steeliness about them today which seemed unopposable. He felt his briefcase almost slip out of his moist hand, and bent his knees to put it on the ground. The slight crouch made him seem so physically powerless that he saw both Harmwell and Wolfitt look away on a kind of shared human impulse to spare him his dignity.

"Give me a moment," he said, and turned from them. He broke the seal on the envelope and pulled out a letter printed on official University notepaper, dated the day before, which read:

Dear Sir Evan,

The University has today received information submitted under the provisions of the Public Interest Disclosure Act 1998. As you know, the Registrar immediately informs me directly as President of Council of all such disclosures.

The University's Public Interest Disclosure Code is used to deal with information received from anyone which expresses a genuine concern that there are reasonable grounds for believing that:

1. a criminal offence has been, is being, or is likely to be committed; or
2. a person has failed, is failing, or is likely to fail to comply with their legal obligations; or
3. a miscarriage of justice has occurred, is occurring, or is likely to occur; or
4. the health and safety of any individual has been, is being, or is likely to be endangered; or
5. the environment has been, is being, or is likely to be damaged; or
6. any of the above are being, or are likely to be, deliberately concealed.

The Code also provides that the identity of the discloser shall not be revealed unless this is essential in any investigation.

The information received today gives rise to genuine concerns that possibilities indicated by (1), (2), (3), (4) and (6) above may have arisen as a result of actions taken by you in your official capacity as Vice Chancellor and/or personally in specific relation to University business.

Given the gravity of these concerns, I have asked the Registrar to establish an internal investigation team which shall report confidentially within 28 days. While this investigation is ongoing, and until further notice, you are suspended from duty on full salary, and should not attend the workplace or engage in any other University business.

You will be required to participate in the investigation in due course, and shall be given further appropriate details as to the nature of the disclosure as part of that participation. Should you feel that the matter requires legal representation, you should retain your own counsel, as the University lawyers cannot be made available to you for these purposes. While there can be no prohibition on your discussing this matter with colleagues, I assure you that it will be dealt with in the strictest confidentiality by the University. You are advised, however, to make no attempt to contact members of senior management likely to be dealing with the case or with members of the investigatory team unless approached.

You should immediately surrender to Mr Harmwell, in his capacity as Chief Security Officer of the University, your University mobile phone and the personal computer provided for your use at your residence at Homestead Park. These items are the property of the University, as is your residence, and Mr Harmwell is authorised hereby, consistent with the terms of your tenancy agreement, to enter your residence without any further warrant in order to retrieve them.

I shall write to you again formally at the earliest opportunity.

Yours sincerely,

Maximilian Knight

President of Council

Chapter Ten

27 October

Covet made three calls in rapid succession. The first was to Asterisk, the second to Buckrack, and the third to McNamara.

An hour and a quarter later, McNamara was sitting on the same couch Buckrack had occupied earlier in the morning, examining Covet with just a hint of curiosity.

"An unusual emergency, you said. But even so, your house in the country? I've never been here before. A call before eight in the morning? Why couldn't we do it in the University? And why me?"

Covet returned his look with an amiable smile. "I wasn't planning to go in today. I got called late last night and the more I thought about the situation the more it seemed necessary to address it instantly. I am sorry about the early call, but it's probably best that we get a head start on this issue. I am grateful that you agreed to come."

McNamara sighed. "Okay," he said, semi-expectantly.

"You remember that young woman I asked you to appoint to a pastoral tutorship in your Hall back at the beginning of this year?"

McNamara sat back on the sofa. "Jane Blake?"

"Yes. How is she doing?"

"As a tutor? She's okay."

"You see much of her? Does she talk to you?"

"Enough."

"How does she seem to you personally? Has she had any problems?"

"What kind of problems?"

Covet smiled again. "I know how you are about confidentiality, Robert, but we've been here before. Nothing is confidential from the Vice Chancellor."

McNamara eyed him sceptically. "If you know how I am about confidentiality, then you know that's not something I agree with. But maybe if you tell me what the concern is involving Jane Blake I might be able to help."

"Fair enough. What I am about to tell you *is* strictly confidential, of course, and needs to stay between us."

McNamara smiled wryly. "I see."

"We had a problem in the School of English over the summer. I don't know if you remember, but Miss Blake was originally registered for a Ph.D. in that School. She submitted a written complaint to the Registrar about a member of staff in the School with whom, apparently, she had become romantically – which is to say sexually – involved. She had broken off the relationship but the member of staff was hounding her, harassing her, becoming quite obnoxious about it."

McNamara felt Covet scanning his expression.

Covet said, "Do you know about that?"

"No," McNamara replied.

"She didn't say anything to you about it? Seek your advice?"

"She didn't discuss any sexual relationship with a member of staff in English with me," McNamara said.

"Did you hear about it from anyone else?"

McNamara shook his head.

130

"It wasn't on the bush telegraph?"

"No," said McNamara. "Was it true?"

"Well, we don't know, and we didn't want to find out," Covet went on. "I decided to try to resolve the problem unofficially. I managed that without too much difficulty. I spoke to Stokes about it, just before his term as Head of English came to an end in July, and we decided that the best way of avoiding embarrassment was to propose that the student transfer to another School. Stokes dealt with the member of staff. There seemed no problem in academic terms, and the student was agreeable to it. I spoke to Cooper in Cultural Studies, and we agreed that Avril Poon could take the student on, although we didn't tell her why, of course. Cooper tipped her off that she would be approached about an internal student transfer, that she should take on the student, and that was it. Miss Blake transferred to Cultural Studies, as you no doubt know, at the beginning of this academic year."

"I see," said McNamara. "So that problem was solved. Obviously something else has happened."

"Yes," said Covet. "Yesterday the student lodged another formal complaint."

"About the same member of staff?"

"No – about Avril Poon."

McNamara raised an eyebrow. "And what was the complaint?"

"Well, this is the thing," said Covet. "The complaint was pretty much identical. Except this time the student claims to have had a sexual relationship with Poon."

McNamara was silent.

"Did you know anything about it?" Covet asked directly.

"What? That she was having a relationship with Poon? Well, everyone knows Poon is a lesbian, but I didn't have

Jane Blake down as gay."

"No, that's not what I was asking." Covet shifted in his seat. "Thing is, I don't believe it. I don't believe it for a second. What I meant was, did you know she was lodging the complaint?"

"No," McNamara replied. "But why don't you believe it?"

"Well, think about it. The student makes a complaint about getting burned over sexual involvement with a male member of staff in summer and then goes pretty much straight off and does the same thing again three months later with a female member? On the face of it, it's preposterous. I'm beginning to think neither of the complaints is true."

"You think she's lying? Why would she do that?"

"No, I think she must be off her bloody head. Nuts. Goo-goo. Loca."

"She doesn't appear to be mentally unbalanced. Not to me, at any rate. A little obsessively observant of decorum, perhaps, but not off her trolley."

Covet clasped his hands. "Look," he said, with seeming reason. "I could let this complaint run its course, have an investigation, and so on. Even if it's not true, that would be very embarrassing for Poon and the Union. The mud will fly."

"With respect," said McNamara, "what do you care about Poon and the Union? I would have thought something like this might make you somewhat gleeful."

"Robert!" Covet exclaimed indignantly. "That's low. I do have some care for the truth, whatever my past conflicts with the Union."

"Well, an investigation will establish the truth. I agree: that's something we all value."

"Yes, but if this got out to the media, the mud would

also stick to the Union. And we could be opening any kind of Pandora's Box here. I am not particularly keen for it to be established that an Associate Professor in the University of Odium, who also happens to be the President of the academic trades union, is having a lesbian affair with a student she supervises, even if it is true. Think of the effect it would have on applications."

"You might get lots more gay girls applying," McNamara joked.

"Yes, I can just see the headlines: 'University of Sapphodium'. But can you help me here, Robert?"

"*Me*?" said McNamara. "Help *you*?"

"I mean us, the University. Surely we have common cause here. You can't possibly wish to see a scandal whipped up around Poon?"

McNamara laughed. "I don't give a damn about Poon. Poon can go to hell for all I care. She's an unprincipled clown and not a very good academic. Books about *Star Trek* and *The Simpsons* and TV show fandom? In fact, I'm not sure I even share your disbelief. She's exactly the kind of person who might have sex with her supervisee. For all I care you can sack her and ship her back to Madras, the more public humiliation the better."

Covet was genuinely surprised. "But that's unfair, Robert. She's been working very cooperatively with us. I don't mean it as an insult to you, or to dredge up things from the past, but relations between the Union and senior management have never been better."

"Precisely," said McNamara. "That's another problem I have with her. When relations between a union and management are so wholesome one should be somewhat worried."

Covet shook his head. "But, Robert, what about partnership? We're all trying to work together for the same thing: a better university."

"Even if this University were made better, it would still be pretty awful, by any measure, because it has people like Poon in it, who have been permitted to carve careers out of their leisure pursuits. You can pretty much get a degree in her department by playing computer games and 'studying' Twitter. But it's not a union's primary role to work for a better university. It's a union's job to represent and further the interests of its members. The two things may coincide. But your idea of a 'better' university and a union's definition are likely to be rather different. Personally, I don't care anyway. I am not even a member of the Union anymore."

"I had heard that, Robert."

McNamara was surprised. "From whom?"

Covet waved his hand. "People talk, Robert. I can't say. But I didn't imagine you had undergone a sudden sea change of political values. From commitment to apathy?"

"I haven't. But then, if you get rid of Poon, who becomes President? Redman. He's way better than her, anyone can tell you that. He has much greater potential as a scholar too."

Each sat back, having reached a discursive stalemate.

Covet made a last effort. "Look, I was hoping you might intervene with this student. You know her. For her own benefit, try to persuade her to withdraw the complaint."

"Why?"

"Because she's mad!"

"That's not been established. And even if she is, mad people have a right to complain. Or there may be method in her madness. Or her madness might have some wonderfully carnivalesque consequences."

"But it could just as easily have been *you* she made

such a complaint about."

McNamara laughed. "Then I would *know* that she *is* mad or lying, wouldn't I?"

Covet said, "I can't believe you're not prepared to help."

McNamara said, "Yes, you can."

As McNamara drove the twelve miles back to Odium in his Ford Mondeo, he was puzzled by his truly profound indifference. His not caring, he realised, did not have even the saving bitter edge of cynicism, the relish of *schadenfreude*, or the self-indulgent pleasure of apathy. The unprecedented call from Covet and the weirdly personal meeting at Homestead Park, in the man's own absurdly opulent paid-for home, hardly registered in his internal seismometers of motivation or involvement. He felt as one can feel when looking out of the windows of a plane, above the clouds, in a certain celestial-seeming zone in which everything below is obscured and its reality removed, the few glimpses of it one is afforded making it seem contourless and transient, something to be passed over, moved beyond. Covet, even in the lap of his own personal luxury, had seemed small and impotent, a kind of helplessness behind his eyes, although McNamara could not summon up the volition to speculate why.

The country roads subsided to the motorway, then there was a mile or two of dual carriageway through the humdrum industrial suburbs of Odium, until he reached University Drive, then the west entrance, with the coat of arms on the green wrought iron gate which read *Ipsa Scientia Potestas Est*. Then, as he drove towards the Trump Building, there were the students. The bells of the tower where he had his office were ringing ten and the young people were moving after the first classes of the day, meeting in gauche physical postures, chatting in painfully un-English rising intonations learned from American TV programmes, their light public embraces too self-conscious and stagey to convey true intimacy, the utterances of "Hi!" upon encountering one another using too elongated a vowel to sound convincingly familiar, their brave attempts to present faces which seemed confident failing to disguise the deep insecurities churning within. Whatever world they occupied, it was not his, or Covet's, or even Redman's. They no doubt naïvely believed that the University, to which these days they paid such high fees from their parents' pockets, was primarily organised around the need to teach them. But the truth was that students were little more than incidental to anyone involved in the managerial politics of a twenty-first century university, just as, with the one troublesome exception of Jane Blake, they hardly figure in any decisive way in the manifold twists and turns of this tale. Students may believe that they have at least bit parts in the show. In truth, they are merely extras.

It had been a long time since McNamara had learned the names of the students in any class he taught. The term "students" merely designated so many empty vessels filled anew each year by a different set of bodies. Their ignorance of virtually everything seemed to deepen as his own wisdom, through experience and scholarship, grew. It had consequently been many years since he had truly prepared for a single class. He knew everything one needed to know to deliver his subject at student level off the top of his head, had heard all the questions and repeated all the answers so many times that he often felt like a juke box merely playing various tunes at the pressing of corresponding buttons. He was a great actor at the lectern, could simulate a passion for knowledge and even spontaneous humour very well. But really, for a long time, it had all been happening on auto-pilot. One day a well programmed android would be able to do it. He was not careless about his teaching, but carefree: hardly any care was in fact required to do it. And perhaps this was also now what was happening in other dimensions of his life. Perhaps it was what the march of age always did, unless some new wholly unexpected challenge or drama arose to force you to rethink your ways and bring you back into a state of worldly engagement. And was it not good, this detachment? Was it not what many holy books described as the ultimate goal of existence?

He parked and entered the Trump Building, walking past Covet's and Asterisk's suite of offices in the west wing, on his way to the clocktower steps. As he entered his office he saw that an envelope had been slipped under the door, with his name written on it. He opened it and took from it a single folded sheet, on which he found a handwritten, anonymous note:

There are listening devices in the following rooms.
(1) Your study in Coolvipe Hall, in the bunch of fake roses between the two bookcases.
(2) In Redman's office in this building, fixed to the underside of his desktop, near the front.
(3) In Poon's office in this building, on the right rear side of the signed picture of Patrick Stewart on the left wall.
These devices are all identical. They are half a centimeter in diameter, and look like a washer made of black rubber with a fine black mesh in the center of the ring. Remove them and keep them in a safe place. There are no other bugs. Further information will follow.

An hour or so later, McNamara caught up with Redman at his home in Maryland Lane.

"Was there one in Poon's office too?" Redman asked.

McNamara nodded. "I've got all three at my house now."

"How did Poon take it?"

"Gobsmacked, I think the word is. I showed her the note, told her I'd been to my study and your office, that we'd found the bugs there, and then we relieved Captain Jean-Luc Picard of his attachment. I didn't have much time to talk to her, she had a class at eleven. I said we'd meet later."

"It has to be Covet, right?"

"Unless there's some MI5 investigation we don't know about."

"I can't believe it. I can't believe they're bugging us."

"Why not? After all, *you're* bugging *them*, aren't you? Jesus, is this what it's come to? 'Odiumgate'? On that score, did you play any of those phone recordings in your office? Could they have heard them?"

"No," Redman reassured. "I only do that here. In fact, while I was waiting for you, I looked through the most recent stuff. Covet called Asterisk this morning before you went there. It showed up on Asterisk's work mobile. You ought to listen."

McNamara raised his hand with a grimace of distaste. "Oh, really? This stuff makes me feel contaminated."

Redman looked him in the eye. "You ought to listen."

He turned to his computer and played the audio file.

ASTERISK: Hello?

COVET: What the fuck, Nigel?

ASTERISK: Er, Vice Chancellor, I wouldn't have taken this call if your ID had shown up. I, I, I... we can't be talking, Vice Chancellor.

COVET: You listen to me, Nigel. What the fuck is going on? Why was I the last to know?

ASTERISK: I can't discuss this, sir.

COVET: You fucking bet you can, you fat prick. Why did you not let me know about this yesterday?

ASTERISK: I couldn't, it's a PID, you know –

COVET: So fucking what? Since when do I not see PIDs before you copy them to Knight?

ASTERISK: But it was a PID about you –

COVET: You miserable fucking fart, Nigel. Isn't that the *very reason* to show it to me?

ASTERISK: But the rules, the Code, I can't. You can't know who it's from.

COVET: The Code? The *rules*? The rules are there for us to apply to other people, you tit, you *arse*. Send me a fucking copy of this thing now!

ASTERISK: [*nervous, gulping*] I can't, sir.

COVET: You can't, Nigel? You *can't*?

ASTERISK: We shouldn't even be communicating.

COVET: You stupid cunt. You *fucking stupid cunt!* Have you any idea how much shit you're in if I'm in it? You imbecile! Tell me who it's from then.

ASTERISK: You know I can't do that. My hands are tied.

[*Silence. Heavy breathing on Covet's end of the conversation.*]

COVET: [*in a low voice*] Listen to me, Nigel, you ungrateful cocksucker. This isn't the end of this matter. You better think about all this carefully and consider what Niagara of piss is about to cascade on your head if you don't listen to me and do exactly what I tell you. But for now, make sure *Avenger* is on that fucking investigation team, do you hear me?

Make sure.

ASTERISK: I can do that, yes.

COVET: You had fucking better. Soon. Today. *Now.*

[*Conversation terminated.*]

McNamara was quiet for a moment. "When was that call?"

Redman checked his screen. "7.37am."

"That was before he called me. He called me about 7.45."

"He didn't use his work phone for that either. I don't have the call."

McNamara thought further. "He told me this morning that Jane Blake had lodged a complaint yesterday."

"About Poon? About them shagging, right? You did tell her when you met her that she could make a complaint."

"Yes, but I got no sense that she was going to do that, and not the very next day."

"Did you mention that to Poon when you saw her?"

"No, she hasn't got a clue. Covet wanted me to persuade Jane Blake to withdraw it. He says he doesn't believe it."

"But this isn't a regular complaint, it's a PID. And it's not about Poon, it's about him."

"But how could Jane Blake make a PID about *him*? She's just a postgrad student. She doesn't even know him."

"Maybe it's a coincidence. She *did* make a complaint, but the PID is from someone else?"

"You think? He calls Asterisk at 7.37 about a PID, is clearly apoplectic about it, then eight minutes later he calls me about something entirely unrelated and much less urgent and asks me to drive out instantly *to his*

140

house? Surely the Blake complaint could have waited if it wasn't the same thing? It would explain why he was so keen to have it withdrawn. The PID must be from her. But how does he know that? Asterisk refused to tell him. Maybe he just guessed?"

"Maybe you can find out from her?"

McNamara shook his head. "We don't know enough. And did you notice the spelling in the note: 'centimeter', 'center'? It's American, not British. And Jane Blake is American."

"You think the note might be from *her*? Do you know her handwriting?"

"No. But she's been in my study, she's been in Poon's office. Whoever put those bugs in needed ready access. I can't explain how she could put one in yours, or why she would put them in any, but this whole thing has become so espionage-parodic I can imagine anything. It's like being in an episode of *Homeland* or something, except with none of the national security implications that make that seem profound. It's a fucking shitty little provincial English university, for God's sake!"

"There's one other thing," Redman said. "He told you he wasn't planning to come in to work today. That's a lie. I know from a couple of previous calls that he had several appointments this morning. Something happened that prevented him going in. That's why he had to get you to go there. My guess is, given the PID – "

"That he's been suspended?"

Redman nodded in agreement. "Which means the PID must be pretty grave."

At that moment, Redman's computer registered with the usual two tone sound that a new email had arrived. He looked at the screen, then back at McNamara. "Another call from Asterisk. Three minutes ago."

McNamara rolled his eyes. "Let's hear it," he said.
Redman pressed play.

BUCKRACK: Yeah?

ASTERISK: Ah, Professor Buckrack. I believe the Vice
Chancellor has spoken to you?

BUCKRACK: Make this quick. Yes, so I know he wants
me on the investigation. When's the meeting?

ASTERISK: 12.30 today. It's been my top priority.
The paperwork is on a collect-and-sign only basis,
from me personally, in my office.

BUCKRACK: Fine. I'll come in now. [*Conversation
terminated.*]

Redman looked at McNamara. "So now we know for
sure who *Avenger* is."

McNamara turned and gazed cogitatively through the
window onto the street. A director would have made a
fine cliffhanger of the moment (even though the
actionless scene itself lacks all suspense), probably by
shooting him in profile from inside the room, fading in a
Sean Callery soundscape, then taking the next shot full-
face-on from the other side of the glass, Redman out of
focus behind McNamara, camera panning slowly away,
the music volume reaching a crescendo as he paused
before whispering the entirely unnecessary confirmation,
"It's Buckrack!"

Chapter Eleven

27 October

"Gentlemen," said Professor Richard Helms, "good afternoon. You have now had time to read the papers. I am sorry that you will have to wait for lunch, but it was necessary, for obvious reasons, that we convene at only a few hours' notice. I am sorry that all we were able to let you have this morning was a copy of the letter of October 26 from the President of Council to the Vice Chancellor but, as you can see from the Public Interest Disclosure document, this is an ultra-sensitive matter on which we have to keep a very tight and highly confidential rein. That is why we are holding these investigatory meetings in camera, without a secretary. I shall be personally responsible for the minutes. I am sorry that you are permitted only to read the paperwork while in this room, and that you cannot take any of the papers away with you, but I should imagine that the nature of their contents makes it obvious why that is so. We are intending to deal with this investigation with utmost despatch, and to make recommendations well in advance of the twenty-eight day deadline which we are obliged to meet. It is obviously a matter which requires a speedy resolution. We must also bear in mind our legal obligations under the 1998 Public

Interest Disclosure Act, which is why, I presume, I as a Professor of Law have been asked to chair the investigatory meetings. You will find our terms of reference on the first page of your papers, and I would like to stress that we are charged only with making recommendations to the University on how it should deal procedurally with the disclosure made by Ms Blake, not with deciding on the case itself: in short, we may recommend that the case be dismissed, pursued by means of another more appropriate procedure, or answered without legal prejudice, and so on. It is for the President of Council to consider our recommendations, although he is not obliged to accept them. This is not a court of law, and the standards of evidence required by a court of law do not apply. We shall weigh the evidence we are given in order to arrive at our recommendations, of course, and, although we shall not be hearing witnesses today, we do have the power to call witnesses and to question them. We can compel employees of the University to attend as witnesses. We can only request that non-employees attend, and they have a right to refuse."

He turned his head to the left and smiled gently at Buckrack. "Now, although most of us know one another, we have not all made the acquaintance of Professor Buckrack, and I am going to suggest some introductions before we get started. I am Professor Richard Helms, Professor Buckrack, but you can call me Dick. Officially I am here as the University Assessor, which is a fancy name for the campus legal bod the University calls in when it wants something dealt with that has a legal angle, but which they don't yet want to pay a practising cash-hungry lawyer to do."

Buckrack smiled back momentarily and then looked at

the other four men seated around the table. "I am Cannon Buckrack. I retired from the US State Department last year, where I worked for most of my career, which also included a period of eight years on the National Security Council. I am finishing a book on intelligence-sharing between the major western powers and, I *also* presume, this was why I was hired on a one-year research contract: I think the intention is to attach my research to a certain School to help float it through next year's Research Excellence exercise." The others chuckled lightly at this. "I think I am a member of this investigatory team because I may be able to help with some of the, er, *trans-Atlantic* issues it raises."

"Thank, you, Cannon. I think there is one particular matter you were looking into with the Registrar just before the meeting, and we'll hear about that in due course." Helms looked expectantly at the others. "Mike, would you?"

The tall, thin, moustachio'd man to Buckrack's left, who had been twitching a pair of bicycle clips on the table in front of him, said affably in an Irish accent, "I am Professor Mike Mansfield, Pro-Vice Chancellor for Teaching and Learning. I can't claim anything as exalted as having been called to the bar like Dick, or having held high government office like you, but in my spare time I do help appoint Justices of the Peace."

At this there were further fond guffaws, of a kind that only university professors are capable of bestowing on one another in their own exclusive company.

The next man took his turn. "Well, as we are all saying a little something of ourselves, according to Google Scholar I am the fifteenth most cited metaphysician in the world! Professor Walt Rostow, Executive Dean of the Faculty of Arts. Pleased to meet you."

And the next: "Professor Pierre Salinger, Deputy Pro-Vice Chancellor for the Student Experience. I'm in the Business School. When I am not helping to forge the entrepreneurs of the future, I run the staff wine-tasting club. You're very welcome to come, if you'd like. Let's talk later."

There were chortles, but none from the last man, who had been unsmiling and unresponsive throughout, mordant, grey, a little hatchet-faced. He said, "I'm Harold K. Johnson, Deputy Vice Chancellor. I don't have any spare time. I help run this place."

This was followed by some shuffling of papers by a few, a polite pause from all, and the placing of Helms's elbows on the table.

"Thank you, gentlemen," he said. "Now to our task. I will begin by summarising the facts of Ms Blake's disclosure, but let me first of all give a little detail about her, solely based on her administrative record. Ms Blake is twenty-three years old. She came to the University in January of this year, having graduated *summa cum laude* from Amherst College, Massachusetts, where she majored in English. She was originally registered in our School of English Studies, where she was supervised by Dr Sergei Krokoff, but transferred for academic reasons at the beginning of this academic year to the School of Cultural and Area Studies, where she is supervised by Dr Avril Poon. Her supervision records are all up to date and show nothing unusual. She was a recipient of a three-year Vice Chancellor's scholarship, and we happen to know for sure that she did meet the Vice Chancellor on at least one occasion, at a reception for beneficiaries of the VC awards in February: there is a group photograph of her with the VC and three other award holders in the March *University Newsletter*.

"Ms Blake claims, however, that she first met the VC almost a year before, in April of last year, in fact, in a hotel bar in Boston, while she was still in her final semester at Amherst, and this is where her own, er, disclosures about herself become, shall we say, *unusual*. She confesses to having financed her education at Amherst by means of regular prostitution. She says that she was essentially 'a call girl with mainly high finance clients' whom she procured in Boston, well away from Amherst, but she also admits to having slept with two of her male professors at Amherst in return for, er, 'academic assistance', by which I take it we mean that they artificially boosted her grades or in some other way ensured that her work was good enough to receive excellent marks. One may wonder why Ms Blake takes the risk of telling us these things. Perhaps she believes that the Public Interest Disclosure provisions prevent any repercussions from being visited upon her as a result of what she discloses, but that is a moot point in English law if the disclosure itself constitutes a confession to criminal activity. I am looking into it. But let us leave that aside for the moment. We may have reason to come back to it later in the investigation, particularly if Ms Blake chooses to present herself as a witness.

"So, Ms Blake claims to have first met the VC in a hotel bar in Boston. She claims that he paid her for sexual services more than once during this visit. She further claims that he returned to Boston in the summer, in July, and resumed with her their illicit liaison on the same financial footing. She then pretty much asseverates that they decided to get their kicks on Route 66. The VC, she says, told her that he had three weeks' holiday, and they spent it together on a road trip across the USA, sharing hotel rooms all the way. In short, he hired her as a sexual companion, something she says she had done with clients several times before. It is not clear from her document whether this was her idea or his, but probably that is of no relevance. The only thing that matters is whether or not it is true.

"It was in Las Vegas, Ms Blake says, 'both of us smashed out on cocaine after a night at the tables', that the VC proposed to her a 'plan' to bring her to England as his, well, I am not sure that 'concubine' would be the precise term, but you've all read the document: the alleged 'plan' was for her to apply as a postgraduate research student to Odium and for him to 'set her up' with a VC scholarship, which was essentially in his gift, in return for ongoing sexual favours. Ms Blake says she accepted this offer, and that it all went smoothly. Thus she ended up as a student here last January, by her account. Their summer road trip ended in Los Angeles, where they went their separate ways. He bought her a ticket back to Boston and himself flew to London. They did not meet again until she came to England, though she claims they kept in touch regularly by phone.

"When she arrived, she says, the VC proposed a new 'plan' with a new tariff of reward. He would give her an additional two thousand US dollars a month in return for an undertaking 'to sleep with no one else he did not ask me to'. His payments to her had hitherto been in cash, but on account of the regularity of these new remittances, she tells us, he set up a pseudonymous PayPal account in US dollars under the name of William Blake (her favourite poet, she explains), so that it would look as if the payments came from her father. She encloses as evidence screen shots of her online US bank account purportedly showing these payments.

"It soon became clear, she wishes us to believe, that

the VC wanted her to put her considerable skills as a courtesan to use in sexually seducing a member of staff, namely Professor McNamara in the School of Politics. The declared motive was revenge: Professor McNamara had recently retired from a long period as President of the local branch of the University and College Union, and the VC wanted payback for all the conflict and trouble Professor McNamara had caused him in the past, and possibly whatever useful information might be revealed in the course of pillow talk. To this end, apparently, the VC again 'set her up' with a residential tutorship in Coolwipe Hall, and gave her the direct mission of bedding Professor McNamara, to whom she would henceforth have regular daily access. Ms Blake expresses some surprise that she was unable to succeed in the planned seduction despite repeated attempts on her part. She goes into some peculiar details about the young woman's art of sexually ensnaring older men in this section of her document, I think to give us a sense of how hard she tried, egged on continually, she wishes us to know, by the VC. Apparently Professor McNamara did not respond to whatever erotic opportunities were being offered him, and after two months she concluded, and told the VC, that it was a lost cause. McNamara was, it seems, a fortress which could not be assailed with success. He survives this bizarre narrative with flying ethical colours, I must say.

"The VC, she goes on, finally accepted her failure, although it exasperated him beyond measure, we learn, 'that Professor McNamara could once more reject something he' – that is, the Vice Chancellor – 'found ineluctably desirable'. She has a way with words, does our Ms Blake, especially when referring to her own sexually charismatic qualities. But the VC then came up, her report has it, with yet another revision to his 'plan'. He wanted to find a way for Ms Blake to seduce the *current* President of the Union, Dr Poon. Ms Blake asserts that she objected vehemently to this idea, and states that this was the point in their relationship when it all began, for her at least, to turn sour. Apparently she did not 'do' women: her prostitutional bent had always been exclusively heterosexual, as it were. But the VC offered two large financial incentives, to be paid up front, which she found it difficult to resist: five thousand dollars to seduce her supervisor in English Studies, Dr Krokoff, an outcome which could then be used as a form of blackmail encouraging him to acquiesce in severing their supervisory relationship, and then another five thousand dollars to have sex with Dr Poon, after she had become the new supervisor. The Krokoff phase, it seems, succeeded almost instantly. Krokoff leapt into bed with her at the first gentle invitation in late April, we are told. The deal with 'Evan', as she calls the Vice Chancellor, was 'for no more than three sexual encounters with Dr Krokoff'. At the same time, Ms Blake proposed to Krokoff a change in her thesis topic which was more suited to Cultural Studies and less amenable to his expertise. Krokoff seemed bemused and discombobulated by this change, but had become almost immediately besotted by her, and so he seemed cooperative. She broke it off with him after the 'third encounter', how much of a strange kind we can only wonder. These three liaisons were apparently carefully spaced out in time to keep Krokoff in a lustfully compliant condition, and the last of them occurred in May. When she told him subsequently that he could expect no more, Krokoff seemed to go instantly mad with sexual deprivation. He pursued her 'like a rabid dog', she writes, 'and with a sexual hunger that threatened almost to make itself public' until the middle of June, when she departed again, she claims, as the VC's companion on another business trip to America. The VC paid for her ticket personally, she adds. She spent some time with her sister in Massachusetts, then joined him again for a re-run of their earlier road trip. She mentions that they laughed hysterically together in Chicago and Albuquerque at the pathetic emails she received from Krokoff during this time, and she attaches those emails to her disclosure. They made me laugh hysterically too, whether or not they are genuine, but, if we can authenticate them, which may not be straightforward as they seem to come from a private email account, I suggest to you that Dr Krokoff's conduct may also be something we must make recommendations about. We shall see.

"After this, it was easy to make an end of Krokoff as supervisor. As he was a mere pawn in the game, and not the prime target of the latest 'plan', the VC apparently did it on the QT. He flew back to England again from Los Angeles, as did she, though separately. He had a bit of hush-hush parley with the two relevant Heads of School, he told her. Krokoff was given a severe talking to and reacted like a frightened rabbit, Dr Poon was softened up in the late summer to expect an approach from Krokoff, heard him out in September without being fully aware of the depths of his depravity, and agreed to what she had already been primed for, that is, she accepted Ms Blake as her transferred doctoral supervisee.

"According to Ms Blake, though innocent thus far, Dr Poon did not even have to be conquered. She started coming on strong at virtually their first meeting, and has been doing so for the last month. It appears that Professor McNamara is the only human being of either sex capable of resisting this young woman's excessive sensual charms. Virtue topples in immediate defeat and bows before them. Perhaps we need to consider carefully whether or not we call her as a witness, lest we too become numbered among the vanquished. But, if we are to believe Ms Blake, it is in her revulsion to Dr Poon that she came to realise the limitations, if not of her attractions, then of her professional capabilities. She simply could not bring herself to commit to an act of lesbian congress. She went back to the VC, she claims, and said she could not go through with it: Dr Poon was disgusting, revolting, a same sex conjunction was beyond her. She even asked him to take back the five thousand dollars she had been paid in advance for the mission. He refused, became overbearing. He purportedly said on one occasion two weeks ago, and I quote: 'You fuck that Chapati bitch now. I want her clitoris on a platter!' Ms Blake refused. There was a standoff between them. Eventually, last week, he relented. She could keep the money, but if she was not going to have sex with Poon, she had to agree to cooperate in framing her for the misdemeanour. Ms Blake would make a formal complaint that *Dr Poon* had seduced *her*: not far from the truth, the VC pointed out, as this was what Poon had been trying to do in any case. The mud which flew from the allegation would stick, and Poon would then, I suppose, be a 'Chapati bitch' in the disciplinary doghouse. The first step in this new manoeuvre was to confide in someone else that there really was a relationship with Poon, and the person the VC chose to receive this fictional confession from Ms Blake was Professor McNamara. Ms Blake reluctantly agreed. She saw McNamara four days ago and told him the lie, apparently under the guise of seeking his avuncular advice. The idea, it transpires, was for the VC then to inveigle McNamara as a witness in the fabricated case against Poon, knowing, as the VC did, that McNamara already had contempt for Poon and would willingly assist in her downfall. But before this could happen, Ms Blake had a sudden, it would seem her first ever, convulsion of conscience. She could not go on like this anymore. She spent a sleepless night, writhing with her demons, and eventually heard the voices of the angels. The next day, October 25, she made an appointment with the Vice Chancellor at noon on the morrow at what she calls their 'usual hotel'. Her intention was to try to persuade him again to give up on framing Poon, but this did not get off the ground, only her feet did: the meeting turned into a routine recreational romp. She went home in a state of some self-loathing, she wishes us to understand, and spent the remainder of the afternoon writing this colourful but literate three thousand word PID then emailed it late that afternoon with the evidence she had to hand, but she says with further evidence to follow, to the Registrar. And this, gentlemen, is how we come to be in possession of the explosive memoir, imagined, loosely based on a true story, or as apparently genuine as the *Confessions* of Rousseau, of Odium's very own Mata Hari."

There was a profound silence in the room, a sealed-off annexe to the Human Resources Department, which was housed in a building nearby. Professor Buckrack looked calmly contemplative. Professor Mansfield toyed anew with his bicycle clips. Professor Rostow puffed a small blast of air through his lips. Professor Salinger put his chin on his chest and opened his eyes wide, darting looks at the others in the room. Professor Johnson grimly twiddled his thumbs for a while and then said, "Do we have any inkling of what the 'other evidence' might be?"

Professor Helms raised his hands to signify the vanity

of idle, legally suspect speculation.

Buckrack said, "It would have to be better than what we've got so far. The JPEGs of bank statements, the email correspondence from Krokoff, both could easily be faked. If there's to be anything else, I'd expect photographs, or videos, or the like. Something that shows them together. There's nothing here that definitively links the two."

Helms, who had just taken a drink of water, cleared his throat. "Not here, no. But we did take the liberty earlier this morning of checking the implied timeline, and the geography. The VC *was* in Boston on business in April last year. We have his hotel bill: the University paid it. It was the hotel she names, the one she said she met him in. We have no details of an American trip in the summer of last year, because that was a personal holiday. But his vacation in the summer just gone was tacked on to a business trip. We paid for the open jaw ticket to Boston, returning from Los Angeles, and again we paid the hotel bill for three nights in Boston: the same hotel, in fact. The bills are all in his name and specify only one guest. So some of the locations and dates she gives for April last year and summer this year tally with our records of his business travel. The question consequently arises, how does a postgraduate student know the VC was in those places at those times, if she was not with him? *Prima facie* there is no reason to consider that she could have been legitimately involved in the Boston business meetings. Of course, even if she did meet him, that does not in itself prove that there was any sexual relationship. We will, of course, ask him if he has an explanation. Cannon, I believe you looked into something with the Registrar just before the meeting?"

"I did," said Buckrack. "On her matriculation form she does list her next of kin as 'William Blake, father'."

"So," Johnson said, "the payments on the bank statement are actually from her father, then?"

Buckrack shook his head. "No. Her father's name is not William Blake." He passed around a photocopied sheet. "She lied. This is the last page of her old American passport, which was a five-year passport she surrendered at renewal two years ago. You can see that she has written the name 'James Arthur Blake' as the first person to contact in case of emergency and identified him as her father. I cross checked the given address in Quincy, Massachusetts, which is also the address stipulated on the matriculation form. A James Arthur Blake lived there until eighteen months ago. He was renting. He was not the owner. He died. Her father is dead. No one called Blake has lived there since."

There was general amazement.

"How on earth did we get this document?" Mansfield asked.

Buckrack shrugged. "As I said, I worked for the US State Department. It took a telephone call to Washington. That's the trans-Atlantic dimension I was referring to."

"Gosh," said Rostow. "I imagined old passports were destroyed."

"Destroyed?" Buckrack echoed. "They're far too important a source of data to be disposed of. In my country, at any rate."

Rostow sat back and whistled. "Can you check the PayPal account the same way?"

"Less easy," said Buckrack. "PayPal is based in San Jose, California, but it's not a US government department, so its records are not so susceptible to immediate examination. We'd need a court order. However, it is interesting that the PayPal payments on this statement seem to come from the European subsidiary in

Luxembourg. That's a pretty strange way for an American citizen to make PayPal payments within the USA. It suggests that the account holder registered the account from within the EU, even though it is specified as a dollar account."

Salinger had been looking around, and as if realising that he was the only one who had not yet contributed to the discussion, took a breath and decided to say, "So those facts tell us?"

Helms said, "They do not tell us anything definite. Ms Blake does not mention the matriculation form in her document. Possibly she forgot. But it suggests, when looked at in the terms established by her other claims, that she wished it to be a matter of false record that she had a familial connection with a William Blake who, that same month, began making payments into her Boston bank account. In other words, it suggests a potentially conspiratorial agreement between her and the person who opened the PayPal account in the name of William Blake, and she claims that person was Sir Evan Covet. The fact that the originating PayPal account was registered in Europe rather than America is consistent with that claim."

Johnson glanced out of the window. "Christ," he whispered.

"But it's not conclusive of any such thing," Buckrack added.

"No, that is true." Helms rallied. "Now, before we go any further, let me describe the legal minefield we are negotiating here under the University's Public Interest Disclosure Code, which was adverted to in the President of Council's letter to the VC. It seems clear that the disclosure before us from Ms Blake does seem to express, and I am quoting again, 'a genuine concern that there are reasonable grounds for believing' that the kind of nefarious things usually dealt with under the Code have taken place, are occurring, or are likely to eventualise. Do we have any alleged criminal offence? Yes, in fact we have several: engagement in prostitution, drug-taking, bribery, and potentially others. Is there any suspicion that a person has failed in his legal obligations? Well, if the VC has conducted himself towards the staff of this institution as Ms Blake says he has, there would seem to be multiple failures of duty of care, as well as favouritism in the award of a scholarship to her: if the latter is not in default of his legal duty, it may nonetheless be construed as yet one more criminal bribe. A miscarriage of justice was also allegedly plotted in respect of Dr Poon, if there was serious intent to 'frame' her for acts of professional misconduct or indiscretion which she did not actually commit. The health and safety of Ms Blake herself was inarguably endangered by the VC if he engaged with her in drug-taking and coerced her into having sex with others. All of the above, if they have been going on for as long as it is suggested they have, inevitably involve concealment, a concealment it is Ms Blake's avowed intention in making her disclosure to end. In fact, the only thing stopping us from having a whole slam dunk across the entire six-item sweep of the PID Code is that no environmental damage, it would seem, has occurred."

"I agree there is a great deal of concern in the terms of the Code," Johnson said. "But as Cannon just noted, we're still in the realm of conjecture. There is nothing solidly associating these two people in what we've seen, other than her claims. She might be clinically insane, hallucinating, or just off on a bender, forgot to take her pills."

"She might," said Helms. "Dare I say we all, as it were,

hope that is so? So you are correct, Harold. I suggest that the next step, therefore, is to agree to reconvene tomorrow and call some witnesses to attend, yes?"

Chapter Twelve

27 October – 29 October

The meeting did not take place the next day, because its necessity was overtaken by events which seemed to speed up time itself, and make the rendition of three days' happenings possible in brief compass only by a kind of verbal montage, whose televisual equivalent might be accompanied by a cheaply licensed song such as "Times of Trouble" by Temple of the Dog.

As the closeted meeting chaired by Helms was getting under way, McNamara, who had returned with Redman to the Trump Building just after noon, opened his office door and found another envelope, this time with only two words written on it:

Release this

Inside was a copy of the letter from the President of Council to the Vice Chancellor. It took only a few minutes for McNamara to find Redman and for them jointly to agree to obey the envelope's imperative. It took less than one more minute for them to decide to keep Poon in the dark and to dissociate the release to the press from the Union. They took fifteen further minutes to compile a list of daily and weekly newspaper education correspondents from the internet, and at lunch time McNamara wandered over to the School of Political Science and, while the School secretary was out to lunch, faxed the document, without any cover sheet or other explanatory gloss, to every one of them from the office's ageing fax machine. News spilling onto newsdesks using such an obsolete technology is a rarity today, and its form made sure it was paid peculiar attention to. By mid-afternoon the calls began to come in to the University press office. By late afternoon Redman's wiretap started registering enquiries from the press office to the Registrar's mobile phone. By the time he arrived home that evening, Redman was able to listen to a series of increasingly manic and petrified calls from Asterisk to everyone, including the President of Council.

By the following morning, which was a Thursday, the campus had become infected with that unique bacillus, the British reporter. To begin with, these were members of the "quality" press, which had already run the story of Covet's suspension in their early editions. But by lunchtime they had produced endospores of the tabloid and TV kind, and all serious hope of holding a further meeting, with witnesses, had to be abandoned. Newsmen and women were crawling all over the campus grounds and, denied access to administrative officials, they were buttonholing anyone and everyone capable of giving a soundbite or a quote: students, librarians, secretaries, academic members of staff, even the benighted Poon, who seized the chance to be recorded for dinner-time news bulletins, on which she was singularly privileged above the various University of Odium *vox pops*, and said that she would be approaching the University as President of the Union to demand further information.

McNamara and Redman at first managed to prevent her from mentioning the bugs they had found in their three offices, but by the afternoon, a couple of interviews already under her belt, fantasising ecstatically of potential celebrity and greater exposure, she offered an exclusive to the BBC and was swept down to London in a chauffeured car. In a state of self-important media intoxication which she considered would make her the envy of her departmental colleagues, ignoring repeated calls from Redman on her mobile, drafting a letter to the Registrar on her laptop, she appeared on *Newsnight* and brandished in front of Emily Maitlis's amused and mischievous eyes a photograph she had taken of the three listening devices. They put her up in the Grange Langham Court Hotel, two minutes from Broadcasting House, where she watched reruns of snippets from her interview on Sky News, and masturbated on the ample double bed in wild self-congratulation.

On the Friday morning, after a sumptuous breakfast but before leaving the hotel, she emailed her letter on Union headed notepaper to the Registrar, with a copy of the photograph, and, knowing well enough how the media works, copied it with unrestrained prodigality to the press. The letter made a formal request under the Freedom of Information Act, asking if the University had purchased the three listening devices, a question the Registrar legally had twenty-one days to respond to, and named McNamara and Redman, without any attempt to gain their consent, as the two other Odiumgate victims besides herself. On the car-ride back to Odium she continued to ignore calls from Redman, but took every other, arranging *en route* an impromptu press conference in the courtyard of the Trump Building, a mere few yards from the Registrar's office. It turned into a gloriously triumphant affair, she thought, after which the media gaggle turned and invaded the building, thronging the corridor outside Asterisk's office, knocking over a security guard and gaining entry, in what, to the police called to eject them, seemed an ironic parody of a seventies-style student occupation. Asterisk decided that it was in his interest to faint, and was filmed leaving the building on an ambulance trolley, flanked by two paramedics and six members of Her Majesty's Constabulary, hounded by a semi-circular scrum of press persons, most holding up portable recorders and taking pictures with their phones.

Buckrack had acted in advance of everyone. On the afternoon of the Wednesday, before the press invasion, while the telephone lines were only mildly warm with the first preliminary enquiries, he returned to Homestead Park and persuaded Covet to leave. Covet had reason to thank him, from the safety of his alternative rural hideaway that Buckrack drove him to, when he saw on TV reporters and paparazzi stationed outside the main gates of Homestead Park the next day. From that moment on he depended on Buckrack entirely, not just for information, but for all feelings of security and protection, as well as advice and judgment. Buckrack felt like the only friend he had in the world. On the first night, over a dinner Buckrack brought in, but which tasted of nothing to Covet, and a similarly supplied bottle of scotch which tasted of something, he confessed what he thought he could no longer withhold and, from what Buckrack had to tell him of Jane Blake's disclosure, he pretty much reckoned was now undeniable: that he had indeed slept with her in America, and twice taken her on holiday, and arranged for her scholarship, and all year had paid her a monthly retainer. He continued to disavow that getting her a tutorship in Coolwipe Hall was a stratagem to entrap McNamara, but three whiskies later he admitted to that too. Two more down the gullet, in a state of glass-smashing despair, he went the whole hog and confessed to the planned and paid-for entrapment of Krokoff and Poon as well. Eventually, in alcohol-fuelled tears, single malt virtually squirting from his eyes, he begged Buckrack to save him, any way, any how. Could he, would he? Buckrack said he'd done it before and could do it again, but it was going to cost. Anything, Covet promised, anything. Buckrack went back to Odium.

The next day, Thursday, Buckrack let himself in to Jane Blake's apartment, informed the moping miss that they had to talk, and removed her once more to his campus house. He did not brutalise her this time. She was too much in terror of him, as she had been for the past week while subject to his surveillance and random un-announced visits, to do anything but comply. He sat her down and also got her a takeaway meal and gave her free access to alcohol. He told her what had been happening. He then proposed a deal by means of which it could all be over, her torment dispelled, and access to her money and identity restored. She grasped at the offer like a saving straw and, in that state of strange intimacy which descends on the vanquished when they are enticed into a compact with a victorious foe, especially given the fact that he was the first person to whom she had ever been able to confess all the putrescent corruptions of her recent life, she felt an odd solidarity with him. As he walked her back to the hall he seemed to her a guardian by her side rather than her nemesis, and to her own amazement she found herself thanking him. She even looked at him, as he prepared to part from her, in a way that she could not but reflexively do, in a mode of invitation. He returned her gaze, voiced his rejection of her unspoken proposition, cursed at her, and turned his back. Instead of reacting with offence at his repulsion, she realised, as she returned to her flat, that she was beginning to admire him. She had come to like McNamara for the same reason. It was now only men who restrained themselves from the temptations she projected whom she could find it in her heart to respect.

The *Newsnight* revelations later that same evening came as a surprise to Buckrack. He was alerted to them by a call from Covet, who gibbered to him on the phone and seemed so convincingly to be having a seizure that Buckrack undertook to drive again the hundred miles or so to Covet's other country residence. By the time he got there Covet was in such a state of alcoholic disorder that there was little Buckrack could do other than take the bottle away from him and put him to bed, himself bunking on the couch near the recently refreshed liquor cabinet. In the late morning on Friday, a monumentally hungover Covet required more tender loving care than one ageing man usually finds it decent to extend to another, but Buckrack gave it. He told Covet that he had a plan for dealing with the Odiumgate situation, instructed him sternly to stay off the booze, and drove all the way back to Odium once more.

Arriving in the mid-afternoon, he discovered that Asterisk had collapsed and been taken to the University Hospital. He went there immediately, encountered the police cordon protecting Asterisk's private room from the press but persuaded one of the officers to tell Asterisk that he needed to see him, and went in upon Asterisk's invitation. Asterisk did not look particularly ill, but he did appear excessively vexed, and, as Buckrack was implicated in the bugging, Asterisk believed he had good reason to help him out of the jam he had been placed in by the Poon letter. This Buckrack promised to do. He spoke to the police again and arranged to have Asterisk transferred home, with the cordon to be relocated to his house. He told Asterisk to check himself out of the hospital, and travelled home with him after they had exited by a service door. On the way, he asked Asterisk where he would find the purchase orders for the listening devices and the pinhead camera and recorder. Asterisk told him his secretary, Alison Stilt, would have all the more recent records. Buckrack said he would remove the relevant documents and that Asterisk should stay home on sick leave until further notice and communicate with no one other than him. Asterisk agreed. Buckrack made him put in one call to Harold K. Johnson, informing him that, with both Covet and Asterisk *hors de combat*, Johnson as Deputy Vice Chancellor was now in charge, and that he could expect a visit from Buckrack.

Buckrack went back to the Trump Building and found Johnson already moving into Covet's grand office. Police and security were everywhere. Johnson badgered him for information about the latest developments, but Buckrack told him that the less he knew the better. He did divulge that he had spoken with Covet and Asterisk and that he was charged with solving the current public crisis. All he needed right then was to be taken to Alison Stilt's office, where Johnson would tell Ms Stilt to cooperate in providing whatever he required. It was better if he asked no questions. Johnson, impressed by Buckrack's decisiveness, concurred.

They went there, and Johnson said the few necessary managerial words to Alison Stilt. He then left, as Buckrack had instructed him to do. Buckrack asked Ms Stilt where recent purchase orders made by the Registrar's department and their associated invoices could be found. She produced two fat document wallets for him, which contained all the relevant paperwork. He asked her to open the Registrar's office and went in there alone with the wallets. Ten minutes later, he emerged and gave them back to her. Then he returned to Johnson once more. He told him to call a press conference later that day, in which he should acknowledge that the Vice Chancellor had been suspended. The important thing was to associate this, as the press were already doing, with Poon's revelations about the listening devices, and to make no mention of the Jane Blake disclosure, of which no one but very senior University managers, the investigation team and Miss Blake had any knowledge. Johnson demurred for some minutes, but was persuaded by Buckrack's reminder of the legal force of the confidentiality with which the disclosure had to be treated. He would hold the press conference. As Buckrack left he told Johnson not to try to contact Covet or Asterisk directly, but to go through him. Johnson said he would.

By this time Redman and McNamara were themselves on the run from the press. The day before, in advance of the media assault on both their unsecured homes which occurred as a consequence of the Poon letter, they had escaped (McNamara with the three listening devices, Redman with his home computer) to Rachel Brace's modest two-bedroomed Bigton abode in Annapolis Drive. McNamara willingly snored through the night with Rachel. Redman set himself up in the spare room, monitoring the activity on Asterisk's phone, although there was little traffic. He guessed that Asterisk was now cautiously conducting whatever conversations he needed to have in person. Then, in the late afternoon of the third day, he picked up Asterisk's call to Johnson warning of Buckrack's imminent visit. Redman discussed it with

McNamara. For over an hour McNamara then chivvied Rachel, who was an initially reluctant but ultimately consenting accomplice, into calling Alison Stilt for any pertinent information. It did not take her long to find out from Alison what she thought Buckrack had come for. It had to be to purloin the purchase orders and invoices for the bugs.

The three watched together, with a sense of rising frustration and defeat, the evening television news, in which, after a seemingly impressive bout of *al fresco* grandstanding by Poon, it was reported that Professor Harold K. Johnson, assuming for the time being the helm of the University of Odium, had promised at a hastily convened press conference that a thorough investigation would begin next week into the Odiumgate charges and confirmed that, until its conclusion, the Vice Chancellor had indeed been suspended. He affirmed, however, that the University was at this stage entirely unaware of any listening devices being planted in its employees' offices and, beyond the claim by Dr Poon and the inconclusive photograph which she had released, it had yet to find any strong evidence which would verify her assertion.

Shortly after the news item ended, McNamara's mobile phone began ringing. He held it up and showed it to Redman. The call was from Poon. He let it ring without answering.

Then Redman's phone rang. He ignored it.

PART FOUR
1 NOVEMBER – 5 NOVEMBER

Chapter Thirteen

1 November – 3 November

The weekend permitted a sense of calm and order to return to the verdant campus grounds of Odium, though McNamara and Redman made no attempt to witness it: both stayed away, as they knew the two-day absence of reporters was an illusion which was at any time likely to be broken. Both had run out of ideas as to how to break it themselves, and were trusting somewhat to their intuitive sense that media wheels, once in motion, take a while to stop. Redman found that a ceasefire descended also on his wiretap. Asterisk's phone was now as dead as Covet's. But the Sundays, tabloid and broadsheet alike, remained alive with rumour and speculation in their synoptic accounts of the drama unfolding in a provincial English university town. Sir Evan Covet was too much an establishment figure for them to leave off encircling the indignity that had befallen him, sniffing for blood, nuzzling in the entrails. The press would almost certainly be back on Monday.

One of the reasons for their return was Professor Drago Baum. He seemed an unlikely source of renewed coverage, but he made himself into one. Baum had been sent to the University's China campus in Chongqing three years before as an Associate Professor. He had managed to establish the germ of a School of Education there, which was as much if not more of a laughing stock among the academic staff of Odium than the home campus's much larger sister School. Educationists are viewed with contempt by the majority of those who like to style themselves scholars, perhaps because the latter hold pedagogy in similar low esteem. The former are besmirched by their association with the training of schoolteachers, an embarrassingly vocational task, and academics generally look down upon schoolteachers, whose ranks are filled, it must be acknowledged, mainly by mediocre graduates who have difficulty finding employment in any other respectable profession.

Baum in person radiated no prepossessing charms which might modify this stereotypical evaluation. He would not have made the needle on a charismometer twitch. He was considered a plodder by his few friends, a drone by the multitude who were indifferent to him, and a Quisling by the two persons he had surprisingly managed to inspire to the heights of bitter enmity. What was worse than all of these, he had grown up in a suburb of Birmingham, a regrettable personal failing to which his thick Brummie accent adverted everyone every time he opened his mouth. These middling qualities, however, were exactly what the senior management of Odium sought in the people it sent to China to make things happen there. And when Baum "delivered" on the Chongqing School of Education (that is, created an administrative edifice which could be given such a name, whatever it was in reality), he had been rewarded with a Chair in the previous November's round of promotions. Afforded the opportunity to label himself Professor of anything he wanted to be Professor of within his field, and after a convivial snifter with the Vice Chancellor in the lobby of the Banyan Tree Hotel in Shanghai, at which he was extremely gratified by the condescension Covet showed towards him, he settled on "Professor of International Education". It did not matter that all his hitherto published work had been on either National Curriculum revisions or the relationship between government education policy and School Examination Boards in England and Wales. It wasn't so much that it accurately described what you did, Covet told him, but what opportunities a title in tune with the *zeitgeist* could be used to generate, and "Professor of International Education" were four words any Vice Chancellor would be happy to see in sequence on his university's website in times like these.

Baum spent the next year trying to write his inaugural lecture, a task incumbent on all new Professors, which had to be delivered in Odium within a year of appointment with the "informed lay person" in mind, as inaugural lectures are by tradition always open to the public. This had proved an excruciating grind, an almost impossible ordeal, in fact, because he knew nothing at all of International Education, which was little more than a slogan used by Odium to euphemise its vaunting overseas ambitions, a term with no scholarly valency, or indeed any accepted real world referent. The lecture was to be delivered on 1 November, exactly three hundred and sixty-four days since his ascension to his Chair, and as late as the week before it he had managed to work up only a few scraps which he considered might be acceptable fare, even to an audience comprised mainly of know-nothings. And then he read on the website of *Times Higher Education* (to which these days he earnestly subscribed) that Professor Sir Evan Covet had been suspended as Vice Chancellor of the University of Odium. Rumour around campus said that there was a major scandal in the making, that Covet's days were over. Covet would not be there to introduce him at his inaugural, or to hear it. Other press sources and those who bore to speak with Baum seemed to confirm the gossip, and there was Avril Poon, on television, clearly throwing down the gauntlet, challenging her fellow academics to arise and build a new Jerusalem on the crumbling ruins of Odiumgate. Why should she get all the limelight? What was she, anyway? An Associate Professor in Cultural Studies? She was no Professor of International Education, that was for sure.

There is a tide in the affairs of men which, taken at the flood, leads on to fortune. Baum had read that in his school days in Dudley, and at this juncture fancied himself something of a Brutus to Covet's Caesar. Poon was merely Casca, the one who had struck the first blow: but he would deliver the fatal stab. It was, he knew, the case that he had nothing much of value to say to his audience as things stood anyway. What he had managed to cobble together was little more than a convenient confection, a panoply of anodyne insights, supported by no authentic knowledge or experience or commitment on his part. How much better to stab with *the truth*. He would – as many another Elizabethan tragedy than the single one he had read put it – seize occasion by the forelock, for she is bald behind. On the Friday before the lecture reporters were not difficult to find on campus, and his insinuation to them, as he put the flier in their hands, that his imminent inaugural lecture might be an event worth attending in the current climate, was winkingly understood.

All of which explains why Professor Harold K.

Johnson, at the end of his first full day as Acting Vice Chancellor, was intimidated to see, as he burbled a laudatory three minute introduction to Professor Drago Baum (written by Baum), that members of the press seemed significantly to outnumber members of the University and of the public in the lecture theatre audience. He did not have time to ponder the unusualness of this, or the reasons why it might be so, because he had somewhere else to be and, in any case, this was a phase already passing strange. Once he had concluded his brief ghost-written encomium, Johnson slipped away. Baum had the floor. He stepped forward, smiled a little nervously, and began.

"Ladies, gentlemen, colleagues, er, members of the press, my lecture tonight is entitled 'International Higher Education in China: Challenges and Solutions'. I have recently returned from a three-year spell at the University of Odium's China campus in Chongqing, where it has been my job, on a practical daily level, as well as on a theoretical plane, informed by many years of experience and scholarship in the field of education, to encounter such challenges and to find solutions to them. I was initially intending to share with you this evening some of the actual challenges I faced and how I successfully solved them. But not only would I be doing you a disservice if I pursued that course, I would also be doing a disservice to *the truth*. And it is the truth about 'International Higher Education in China' – a phrase which in reality denotes the commercial invasion of British universities such as this one into the backward Chinese educational marketplace in pursuit of enlarged income from abroad and political clout at home – which I wish to avail you of tonight. So let me commence.

"British universities in China are running a racket.

There is no other word for it. The imperatives are fundamentally monetary, not educational, and the satisfaction of these imperatives is ultimately at the root of every questionable decision taken, every amateur appointment made, every backstairs manoeuvre executed, every policy of the home institution flouted, every academic standard allowed to go by the board, and every corrupt genuflection given to a dictatorial, undemocratic, morally retrograde communist regime. When I say 'International Higher Education in China' I mean you to understand that all these accommodations, taken together, are really what the term denotes, but which it, with its seeming beneficent aura, disguises. You might have thought I was going to talk on this occasion about the problems and dilemmas involved in teaching non-British students. I am not. I am going to describe to you instead how we crucify our cherished educational aims at the altar of Mammon. That is what, under the auspices of 'International Higher Education', British universities are now doing in China.

"How do we do it? Well, let us start at the very beginning of the process. You have a meeting with ministers of the British Cabinet at which you talk their language, namely the language of business and trade. Education, in this parlance, is an exported good: it shows up positively on our balance of payments. While you are not the first British educational institution to float the idea of stepping foot in China (in fact, you are simply trying to jump on the bandwagon because of the seeming public *coup* performed by the first one which did), you are unambiguously reassured, by twinkling ministerial eyes in the cocktail reception which follows in Whitehall, that a knighthood is pretty much in the bag for you personally if you see it through. The Foreign Office finds you, with amazing speed, a highly placed Chinese businessman, whose English is rudimentary but whose pull in Beijing is considerable, and you make him your Chancellor for five years – an honorary position, to be sure, but one which allows you to assign him flunkies and considerable expenses on his frequent trips to the UK, whose prestige, moreover, he himself can use as a kind of personal currency back home. No matter how much this costs in merely financial terms, it pays off in manifold ways. He takes care of all the necessary preliminary machinery, and gratifyingly reports that, as far as Beijing is concerned, you are pushing on an open door. All you need to be prepared to do is follow the rules stipulated by the men who will be behind that door.

"The first thing these men tell you, with a huge portrait of Chairman Mao behind them, is that you will not choose the city in which your Chinese campus will be situated: they will. Nor will you own the land or have control over the buildings, the architecture, the student residences, or the on-site services: these will be the remit of an 'educational corporation'. That body will hold a seventy per cent stake in 'the venture'. You will have only thirty per cent, although you will be permitted to cream off one tenth of the operating profit from that thirty per cent and return it to the UK home institution.

"There will be no equal opportunities in student recruitment. You will be able to accept applications directly from international students, but not from Chinese nationals: applications from them will be accepted only from provinces the Chinese Ministry of Education deems from time to time eligible, the Ministry will determine whether or not the students meet the agreed criteria for entry, and will then allocate students, acting as your proxy, to you. In particular, although it is understood that you are an exclusively English language institution, you will not make the same demands of competence in English from Chinese nationals, at either undergraduate or post-graduate levels, that you impose on successful international entrants, but will provide a 'foundation year' in which Chinese students lacking in this regard shall be taught English by you to a presumably sufficient standard for them to be able to continue. Even then, you shall not, at this continuation stage or any other time, subject these Chinese students to objective English language proficiency testing of the IELTS or TOEFL kind. It is an assumption that no more than two per cent of students shall ever fail to proceed in any one annual cohort.

"Your institution will accept a Communist Party official on its Management Board, in reality a kind of ideological overlord whose officially described function will be 'Ministry of Education Liaison', and who may at times act as your institution's advocate, or smooth out any difficulties which may arise with Chinese state officialdom you cannot be expected to understand, but whose role need not be too explicitly stated: it is understood that his word is final on all matters. He will organise the Party members among the student body. You will also comply with Chinese government requirements that all Chinese (but not international) students shall be subject to compulsory extra-curricular physical and political education, that they shall be assessed in these two areas, and that they must perform adequately in them to survive in the institution. If they do not, they will be excluded.

"This last is the first matter you baulk at, and the officials no doubt smile that it has taken you this long, because it is in fact their penultimate demand (the final one is that you must agree to accept the censored Chinese internet and make no effort to circumvent its imposed constraints). You explain that personally you are made of the stuff of *realpolitik*, but your own staff back at home will find it difficult to approve these compulsions, particularly the one about 'political education'. It will be viewed by them as the forced instilling of dogmatic Marxist propaganda, and will never be accepted at curriculum planning stage. They explain that it is non-negotiable within the legal framework of the Chinese state, but experience has taught them that this has been an ideological stumbling block before, and they have therefore devised a method that means it requires no approval: the instruction in both physical and political education will take place off campus and need therefore appear in no curriculum presented to your home institution for endorsement. It is simply necessary that you know it will take place. At this you wave your hand and agree. In short, you signal no opposition to everything they formally require of you.

"What follows from this acquiescence is an institution which, almost from the get-go, resembles nothing like the British one, but bears its name and awards its degrees. Because you have relinquished any say in the running of on-site buildings and services, you discover that students are racially segregated by the 'educational corporation' which commandeers the infrastructure. The Chinese students are domiciled in single sex halls of residence in which each dormitory, a room with two sets of bunk beds and a single toilet and shower, is shared among four students. Communist Party student members are distributed evenly throughout these residential blocks to form a supervisory cadre. The Chinese halls are closed at 11pm each night, latecomers being refused entry, and there is a communal lights out at midnight, when the internet is also disconnected, until 7am. The international students reside in their own separate blocks, which are open twenty-four hours a day: they have single occupancy rooms with *en suite* bathrooms and uninterrupted (though still censored) internet access.

"You discover that most of the Chinese students at entry, including postgraduates, have little or no English. You are the most expensive university in the whole of mainland China and they feel privileged to be in a prestigious foreign institution, but hardly any of them can express such a statement, using such words, in anything but Chinese. The struggle to teach them, in one foundation year, enough English to be able to meet the demands of even a typical first-year British university curriculum in any subject is clearly doomed from the beginning. But you are not permitted to test their English proficiency by any objective means at the end of the year, and remember, nor are you permitted to fail more than two per cent of them. In actuality, nearly everyone passes, by a combination, during this foundation year, of turning a blind eye to their rampant plagiarism and teaching them that 'paraphrase' of an original is the replacement of every sixth word by a synonym. Not that they ever really get to know what a synonym is: in my three years in Chongqing I never saw a student with a half-decent English language dictionary, never mind a thesaurus. Once they discover that libertine approaches to the assessment of their entirely derivative (or more accurately duplicative) work are acceptable to you, these methods of cheating and charlatanry quickly become their engrained reflex habits.

"The better students in the foundation year tend to pass by copying high school essays written in Chinese from a site called Wenku Baidu, then running these through Google Translate. The results are outlandish gibberish in English, but they do not give the appearance of being plagiarised, even though they are, and the students manage to get marks averaging in the mid-fifties. The same essays submitted in Odium itself would be lucky to receive what we call a 'soft fail' – that is, they would get a mark between thirty and thirty-nine. The more mediocre students plagiarise English internet sources entirely and tend mechanically to replace occasional words or phrases with (usually incorrect or hilariously inept) English alternatives. Their mixture of cut-and-paste English with improvised Chinglish receives marks averaging in the high forties. In Odium this kind of work would be a 'hard fail', that is, the mark would be below thirty. The weakest students of all simply submit entirely plagiarised pap, which, though understandable as English, is often grossly nonsensical in a different way, as it is usually not material of any academic kind that is being plagiarised, but magazines, trashy websites, newspapers, general discursive detritus. You might wonder why work of this nature, which would receive a zero mark in Odium and potentially lead to removal of the student from the University on grounds that its submission is academic misconduct, can receive marks averaging in the low forties in Chongqing. Well, the line is obvious: you must hold to the *diktat* that no more than two per cent of students can be failed. You cannot with a clear conscience, however, reward outright plagiarism. The solution is ingenious, and it is in devising this solution that you truly demonstrate your ability to cultivate the Chinese way of doing things. You ensure that such work is *never categorised as plagiarism*. How do you do this? Firstly, you ensure that suspected cases of plagiarism must be referred for adjudication to Heads of School by individual tutors. Before the tutors are allowed to refer, however, you make the burden of forensic proof intensely demanding of detail and subject to a highly bureaucratic procedure which must be followed separately for each individual student. With classes of more than two hundred students, in which perhaps over fifty per cent have rather blatantly committed plagiarism, this is clearly impossible. The staff thus do not refer, because they cannot write one hundred or more such referrals within the twenty-one day time period inflexibly set for marking students' work. When the tutors complain about the injustice of this procedure, the Head of School has a word in their ear and tells them they can do anything they like with work strongly suspected of plagiarism as long as they don't fail it outright, because students are not permitted to appeal against their marks. The tutors thus give the lowest marks they can get away with: forty or slightly above.

"Some students' English does improve as they progress, but stumblingly, haltingly, and seldom gets beyond the basics, with only a few stories of heroic individual accomplishment. Over a period staff become inured, not simply to mediocrity (there is enough of that among students here in Odium itself) but to the downright inanity, stupidity and gormlessness of Chinglish. Virtually every teaching session at Chongqing, one colleague told me, is like taking a remedial class in any subject at an English comprehensive secondary school, minus the bad behaviour. Eventually, staff begin to disregard the fact that the work is mostly incoherent drivel and perform a rough translation (Chinglish to English) on the fly in their heads as they mark it, then give a mark based on what it would have looked like in

182

some alternative non-existent Chinglish-is-English uni-verse. I have seen Ph.D. degrees awarded in Chongqing for theses which seem to have been written by an average British thirteen-year-old (you will note that all of these theses have been excluded from the UK online repository of doctoral theses, and for good reason). How, you ask yourself, do staff put up with it? Well, it must be understood that only a handful of these staff would be able to hold down an academic job in Odium itself. For the most part they are the usual foreign legion desperados one finds on the English Language Teaching or International Schools circuit, or star-crossed Ph.D. graduates who have found themselves unemployable in the UK, Australia, Singapore, Canada or the USA. Some of them do not have English as a first language either. Hardly any have ever worked in a UK institution of higher education. Those who can find a job elsewhere get the earliest flight out. Those who cannot remain. They are easily whipped into compliant local shape by a small tier of (no more than a couple of dozen) senior managers seconded from Odium with very hard-nosed business purposes in mind. These managers also ensure that conscientious Heads of School in Odium who try to interfere are foiled in their attempts to rectify the shocking quality problems they witness there. The final results are almost cosmically staggering. The universal grade average of students in Chongqing, hardly any of whom can write a single fully grammatical sentence in English at graduation, is a mere nine percentage points below that of students in Odium.

"In brief, the typical UK university in China is like a decayed pineapple, entirely rotten from the inside, whose outer husk is nonetheless maintained to give the illusion that it is edible. A persuasive fruiterer is still able to sell such a pineapple. Perhaps, however, there is a better analogy. The University of Odium at Chongqing is not really the University of Odium at all, but is maybe best understood as a franchise operation, a local mutant zombie relation of the real thing, like the KFCs and McDonalds and Starbucks of the kind you see in the untrendy shopping malls now rising from the filthy streets of dilapidated Chongqing itself..."

He went on for much longer, but this was food and drink enough for the assembled press. The lecture ended with a few cheers and some applause, but not from the reporters or photographers, whose hands were too busy with their mobile phones or cameras. They surrounded a jubilantly smiling Drago Baum at the close, grasping copies of the text of his lecture which he had prepared in advance to thrust into their outreaching palms, a lecture reprinted entire in one daily newspaper the following day, in excerpts in many others, beside an inevitable picture of him in professorial lecturing posture, a caption running underneath like "Baum: 'British universities in China are running a racket'", or "Drago Baum explaining how the University of Odium is 'best understood as a franchise operation'".

Baum read all of this stunning and copious coverage the following day, surrounded by a small mountain of newsprint, with swelling heart and rising mojo. For the first time ever he felt an enormous sense of pride in his own courage and daring and achievement, at least in so far as they could be measured in front of his very eyes by sensational column inches. His gamble had paid off. Cometh the hour, cometh the man. He found it hard to imagine that he would ever feel this good again throughout the remainder of his life. He was right. It was while he was looking, with a golden afterglow still tingling in his veins, at his picture in the *The Independent* ("'We crucify our cherished educational aims at the altar of Mammon,' Professor Baum stated") that Harold K. Johnson called him and fired him, without notice, for bringing the University into disrepute.

"You stupid ass, Baum," he said. "Have you any idea what you've done? Do you really think the Chinese will take all that crap sitting down? Did you really think you were big enough to get away with it? Can you imagine what kind of shit storm is coming our way from out East? You witless bastard!"

The same newspapers reported on the morrow the suspected suicide of Drago Baum. It appeared that he had carbon monoxided himself in his own garage one or two hours after Johnson called, a year to the day since he had become a full professor, an academic made man. His death finally did it for Johnson too. That afternoon he was summarily relieved of his duties both as Acting Vice Chancellor and Deputy Vice Chancellor, and sent back in shame to his ordinary post in his academic School. The Foreign Office was kicking up a stink. The Chinese Ambassador had been to see them. The lecture Johnson had introduced had caused a diplomatic incident, and the member of staff who gave it had now gone and topped himself into the bargain.

"Jesus, Johnson," the President of Council expostulated in the Vice Chancellor's magnificent office. "Have you any notion what you've officiated over? What you've allowed to take place? Do you seriously think we can withstand yet another scandal? Why did you not stay and stop him giving the bloody talk as soon as it got out of order, which was about one minute in? But no, you buggered off and the idiot went on an insane bender anti-Chink monologue, in front of all the newspapers of the land and an ITN news crew. The University of Odium is on its way to hell in a public handcart, and you've given it a push!"

Chapter Fourteen

3 November – 5 November

The University of Odium proved to be a Hydra with only three heads. Once those of Covet, Asterisk and Johnson had been lopped off and put into cold storage, no one else dared hazard his mazard. Maximilian Knight, as President of Council, convened an emergency meeting of what remained of the Management Board, but discovered that this simply precipitated among more than half of the Pro-Vice Chancellors a spree of instant resignations from their senior administrative roles in preparation for incipient flights back, *à la* Johnson, to the relative obscurity of their Schools and Departments. Even those who were not thrusting termination notices into his hands were unwilling to step any closer to the toxic spill which had resulted from the triple decapitation. Knight got the message, called the Secretary of State for Education, and told her that he too was tendering his resignation from his voluntary position, with immediate effect. The rat which remains on the sinking ship is a stupid rat.

In previous periods more carnival-inclined or more anarchistically minded than the twenty-first century has yet been able to emulate or imitate, students and staff of a modern university most probably would have revelled in the radical opportunities thrown up by even the briefest disorder of things. This did not turn out to be so at Odium. There were no teach-ins or flowerful staff-student assemblies of any other kind. Nothing was perceived as being up for grabs. Instead, the immediate reaction to media revelations of the power vacuum, as they rippled through the ranks of middle management, was to abdicate all assigned responsibility. If there was no pretender to the throne, there was no point in pretending there any longer was a throne. Many Heads of School simply stayed away to listen to how things unfolded on the Radio 4 news.

Poon, who had been feeling sidelined for days by the Baum affair, checked the Union records and, though he was predictably not a member, decided that it was a useful pretext for an emergency general meeting of the Union nonetheless. Redman did not attend, but hundreds of members of staff abandoned their lectures and seminars at three in the afternoon to do so. The meeting was a real humdinger, with a bigger turnout than anyone could remember, plus there were lots of TV cameras, which encouraged unprecedented displays of performative militancy throughout the proceedings. No one exceeded Poon, at the podium, in this mode. One had to admire her daring in calculating the chances that a motion in favour of an immediate *en masse* staff walkout would succeed. But her stock after Odiumgate was high, and she had turned off her mobile so that frantic calls from Union HQ, which wished to impress upon her that a walkout without a formal ballot would be entirely illegal, should be ignored. Her motion carried the day, and the entire nation witnessed on TV the consequent *debouche-ment* from campus of the loudest phalanx of Ph.D.

holders ever seen in the recorded history of the world. Then they all went home, and left the stage even more bare. Poon's diary filled up quickly with new media engagements. No one was available to comment on the management side.

The Odium Students' Union, by comparison with the one represented by Poon, had it ever been a political entity, was never one under Covet. He had kept it well financed (which was not in institutional terms very expensive) in return for a "partnership" in which it stuck to organising social rather than political events. He mixed with its elected officers many more times a year than he had ever deigned to meet with McNamara or Poon or Redman, and if the SU President did not exactly have a seat at his table she was generally invited to lick up the crumbs which he let fall from it in her direction. The current SU President, Ivy Littletot, was, as a matter of genuine strong emotion, scandalised by the reported suspension of Covet, for it also eclipsed whatever of his reflected glory she could bedazzle others with. She had in fact quickly organised a student petition for his imm- ediate reinstatement, and more attention would have been paid to it had Ivy's stats been better on ratemash. com. As things stood, that site did not have her down as one of the "hotter" female Odiumites. There was only one vote against her name, in fact, and she had put it there herself. But when Poon's walkout was announced a different light bulb sparked into life in Ivy's head which might galvanise the campaign for the return of the Vice Chancellor. She drew up a template email for students to send to the Office of the Independent Adjudicator, in which they could complain about every single class they missed. Students now slept gratefully late, and extended their gratitude to their university by an endeavour (in what remained of the day) consisting solely of filling out the blanks in this template and sending it to the OIA every time they heard from someone sent to recce that the convener or seminar tutor had failed to show. By the second morning following the Wednesday walkout, a large updatable display was already in the eyeline of anyone ascending the steps to the Students' Union, which multiplied the number of cancelled classes by a wild estimate of the number of students to whom they were intended to cater: "25,420 STUDENTS DENIED THEIR RIGHT TO TEACHING YESTERDAY". In short, the student body seemed to erupt into a spontaneous consumer-style revolt. On the same day, the national press let everyone know, the OIA's server crashed.

McNamara and Redman avoided reporters by taking self-certified sick leave on the Monday, Tuesday and Wednesday, during which they remained under voluntary house arrest at Rachel Brace's. But the walkout faced them with a dilemma. If they stayed away, they would be deemed to be participants in it. If they did not remain in their sanctuary, but ventured into the fray, there was no telling what might happen. McNamara, who had found the last few days quite sexually enchanting and was even considering asking Rachel to move in with him on the strength of how well they cohabited, was in perhaps too mellow a mood to judge the situation aright. He made the mistake, over evening drinks with Redman, of committing himself to a five-minute monologue about "dukkha" – the Buddhist concept of "suffering" or "unsatisfactoriness" caused by a discrepancy between the reality witnessed and one's expectations of it – in the service of an impromptu argument that they should sit tight. Before he could finish, Redman lost the rag and told him (in not so many words) that he could stay where he was and chant his sutras and mantras asking Buddha to turn the fucking Dharma wheel if he liked, but he'd be damned if he was not going to clutch and cling in a worldly way to a proper sense of truth and right, however imaginary these seemed from the shade of the Bodhi tree.

Redman thus went in to teach his classes on the Thursday morning, and in doing so almost lost the real rags from off his back. Reporters massed around him outside the entrance to the Trump Building, barking leading questions and inviting him to fellate their out-thrust microphones. It was several minutes before police and security could clear a passage for him to enter, and when he got to the seminar room, late, he was dumbfounded to find only one of the students in the class, Betsy Pankin, waiting for him. Betsy seemed equally surprised and a little disappointed. She had only come, she explained, so that she could report his absence to the others, and they could all send yet another batch of aggrieved emails to the OIA. She had not prepared. He wasn't going to subject her to an hour of one-to-one teaching, was he? No, he said, he wasn't, and she could do whatever she liked. Then he threw open the ground floor window and escaped into the service road at the rear of the building, leapt over the adjacent wall, and retreated on foot back to Rachel's. McNamara met him with a brahm-avihāratic smile.

On the Friday morning McNamara retreated to Rachel's upstairs toilet with a newspaper the early-rising Redman had passed to him with a sour face and rolling eyes. There, with his boxer shorts around his ankles and his elbows on his knees, he reluctantly permitted his increasingly luminous mind to be defiled by a long feature entitled "The Odious University" by one "Melanie Oldtosh, Education Correspondent":

191

Whatever one may think of Professor Sir Evan Covet, the abrasive and outspoken Vice Chancellor of the University of Odium, it has to be acknowledged that, in less than two weeks without him, the institution he has led for thirteen years has plunged headlong into a spectacular meltdown, and one which may yet change the face of higher education in Britain as we know it.

Sir Evan, who once attracted the approbation of Margaret Thatcher and the ridicule of his colleagues for suggesting that UK universities ought to be privatised, was suspended on full pay by the University on October 27 after an anonymous whistle-blower alerted it to legal and other concerns over his professional conduct.

The nature of these concerns remains officially unconfirmed, but they have been linked to his alleged role in the bugging of the offices of two officials and one ex-official of the University and College Union (UCU). Dr Avril Poon, President of the Odium branch of UCU, and one of the academics who claims her office was bugged, filed a Freedom of Information request last Friday on the part of UCU, seeking confirmation from the University as to whether it had purchased listening devices.

The two other purported victims of bugging are Professor Robert McNamara and Dr James Redman. Neither has been available for comment this week, although Dr Redman, who is the UCU Vice-President, reported for work yesterday in what is being seen as open disapproval of the unofficial action of the Union members he represents. He appeared so indignant and affronted by reporters, however, that he refused to answer any of their questions.

The University has two more weeks to respond to

Dr Poon's FOI request, and has stated that an investigation is under way. Until that investigation makes its recommendations, it seems that the University intends to remain tight-lipped over "Odiumgate", as it has inevitably been dubbed.

One problem may be that there are hardly any senior managers remaining at Odium who might make any public comment. Sir Evan has been in hiding since news of the Public Interest Disclosure hit the headlines. On the day Dr Poon filed UCU's FOI request, Odium's Registrar, Dr Nigel Asterisk, took official sick leave after collapsing in front of reporters who had invaded his office, and he has not yet returned to work.

The Deputy Vice Chancellor, Professor Harold K. Johnson, lasted just a few days before he and several members of the University Management Board resigned their administrative positions on Wednesday. The same day saw the voluntary departure of Maximilian Knight, President of the University of Odium Council, whose letter to Sir Evan in October first set the train of recent events in motion.

The reason for the spate of managerial resignations earlier this week was a blistering indictment in a public lecture on Monday evening – by its own Drago Baum, Professor of International Higher Education – of the University's operation in Chongqing, China, where it has one of its overseas campuses. Among many other accusations levelled by Professor Baum was the charge that Chinese students in Chongqing suffer compulsory indoctrination with Communist Party propaganda as part of their studies.

The Chinese Ambassador made a formal complaint to the Foreign Office about the "anti-Chinese" nature of the lecture. Professor Baum was fired on Tuesday, and his body was found later the same day in what appears to have been a suicide. Coming on top of the "Odiumgate" accusations, Professor Baum's death seems to have been the final catalyst for the University's vertiginous descent into turmoil.

On Wednesday afternoon, a mass meeting of local members of UCU, which considered the bugging allegations and the sacking and death of Professor Baum, ended in an unofficial walkout. Many non-unionised members of academic staff, seemingly in sympathy with the strikers, have also refused to attend work for the remainder of this week.

Lecture theatres and seminar rooms at Odium have, for the most part, stood empty since Wednesday afternoon, and there seems no end to the unofficial action in sight, despite the fact that the national office of UCU has dissociated itself from the walkout and urged its members to return.

Students yesterday were collectively appalled by the failure of academic staff to turn up for classes, and have begun filing mass complaints to the Office of the Independent Adjudicator, the higher education watch-dog.

The Secretary of State for Education, Dr Shirley Tang, was asked questions about the Odium situation yesterday in the House of Commons. Her responses took everyone, apparently even the seemingly prepped questioners of her own party, by surprise.

She informed the House that matters would not be sufficiently righted simply by taking legal action to force Odium lecturers back to work, and that she had decided, in consultation with the Prime Minister, on "more radical measures". This led to disbelieving obstreperousness from the Opposition benches, including a speech by one backbencher which contained mock Mandarin phrases.

Dr Tang, who is British Chinese, ignored the raillery. She went on to announce that she had appointed Professor Norbert Conquest as interim Acting Vice Chancellor of Odium until the resolution of the crisis. Professor Conquest is currently Vice Chancellor of the University of Surleighwick, a mere thirty miles north of Odium, and is known in academic circles as an economist of the unfettered free market.

What the "radical measures" are that he might put in place became clearer yesterday afternoon when he arrived in Odium and issued a statement saying that his own university would be opening its doors to Odium students who wished to transfer permanently into comparable degree courses at Surleighwick from the beginning of next semester. Odium students who exercise the option will also be offered financial compensation in the form of reduced tuition fees at Surleighwick, his press release added.

The announcement was greeted with scorn, and rejected as a bluff by Dr Poon, architect of the unofficial walkout, during an interview with her on *Channel 4 News* yesterday evening. By contrast, the Odium Students' Union President, Ms Ivy Littletot, featured on the same programme, said it was great news for Odium students, who were being denied value for money and deserved to have such an alternative. She predicted that many Odium students would take up Professor Conquest's offer.

No one in senior management at Odium was available to comment on Professor Conquest's statement, although one Associate Professor, who wished not to be identified, wondered if he would be willing to take on members of Odium's academic staff as well.

Reaction from other university Vice Chancellors, however, has been immediately explosive. One, who also declined to be named, said that the entire affair was an example of cynical opportunism on the part of government to force the hand of the HE sector into dog-eat-dog competition for students. Another, similarly off the record, claimed that Professor Conquest's behaviour was not that of a caretaker, but more that of a corporate raider, a liquidator, or an asset stripper.

However, he agreed with other VCs, who said without hesitation that if the Surleighwick offer were to be confirmed then they too would consider making similar approaches to the discontented students of Odium, and put equivalent transfer systems in place in their own universities without delay.

There can little doubt that Professor Conquest's offer is serious. An email to all Odium students yesterday evening indicated that an application system for those wishing to transfer to Surleighwick would be up and running by the middle of next week.

In an unusual departure from typical BBC practice, two scheduled guests were dropped at the last minute from yesterday's live *Question Time* programme so that Drs Poon and Tang could face one another from either end of the debating table. Dr Poon rancorously repeated her charge that the Surleighwick initiative was a ploy to blackmail striking Odium staff back to work.

Rather more coolly, Dr Tang replied, "Students no

longer care if you go back to work, now they know you can no longer treat them as a captive market. You are about to find out that student mobility means more than sending students for an exchange year to your campus in China."

At the end of a tumultuous fortnight, then, the University of Odium appears to be a dying animal eyeing a flock of expectant hungry buzzards gathering steadily overhead. Students are next week likely to initiate what has never been seen before in UK higher education, something like the equivalent of an academic run on the bank.

If Professor Sir Evan Covet wishes to save his university from the gathering gang of predators, he had better come out of hiding this weekend.

McNamara finished reading the article in something of a *dwalm*, a word he had first heard during his childhood in Scotland. His head was dazed, but so was his left leg. Pins and needles were radiating up and down its lower half, and his foot was so benumbed that the floor beneath it seemed to give and slip away beneath him. He rested his arm on the sink and tilted his weight to the right. He stamped his left sole lightly on the wooden planking, and a disorientating electrical charge seemed to go off in it, rising rapidly all the way to the knee. He winced. It was strange that such light contact with the world could produce such discomfort, and even stranger that something that could not actually be called pain seemed even less desirable than it. He hobbled downstairs, holding on to the banister, noting with relief that the nervous repercussions reduced to lesser and lesser tingles with each step. By the time he reached Rachel Brace's living room he was no longer limping.

Redman was holding a cup of coffee and staring out of the window. He turned and looked at McNamara.

"Poon's fifteen minutes of fame," McNamara shrugged, gesturing at the newspaper. "Nearly over, I suspect."

Redman did not answer at once. Then he said, "Whether we do something or nothing, things go against us."

"Poon's not exactly been doing nothing," said McNamara.

"I don't mean Poon. I mean you and me."

"We went public with Knight's letter to Covet, didn't we?"

"Yes," said Redman. "And all that did was bring vampires onto campus, to whom Poon offered herself as a willing human sacrifice. If we hadn't done that, the entire matter would have been dealt with internally."

"Maybe not. There was Baum, after all. No one could have predicted that."

"Baum? I knew him before he went to China. He was a worm, and not the sort that turns. I can't prove it, call it intuition, but I suspect he was playing to the press gallery. If that's true, it was also avoidable."

"Another fifteen minutes of fame, then, and more abruptly terminated. But don't you at least savour the fact that he blew the gaff on China?"

"Yes, but to what end? A decimated executive, a mass flight from the field? Half of Management Board vacated, and then the Union ran away too, and now the students are preparing to exit. It's like a boxing match where the two fighters leap over the ropes and go back to their dressing rooms, then the audience drifts home, leaving just the referee – Norbert Conquest – standing in the ring, declaring himself the winner. It's rich. I was meant to be defending the interests of Union members. We end up in a situation in which lots of them may be out of their jobs by February and the whole sector goes into government sponsored competitive freefall. What a victory!"

"Hardly your fault," McNamara consoled. "Things have a habit of snowballing."

"Maybe not," agreed Redman. "But what I actually *tried* to do, the monitoring of Tweedledum's and Tweedledee's phone calls, I had such hopes it would be revelatory, conclusive, and it came to nothing. It was a dry well."

"It helped us interpret things a little better. We know Buckrack probably filched the invoices for the bugs, for example."

"But what good is that? It's only knowledge of how we were defeated. It *changes* nothing. We can't use it."

McNamara sat down. "I've often found that succeeding in changing things for the political good leads to unanticipated consequences which are bad. Call me a pessimist, if you will."

"No," said Redman. "I don't think you're a pessimist. I'm beginning to think you're just *correct*. But I can't reconcile myself to ignoring what's wrong the way you do."

"Don't," said McNamara. "That's not it at all. I don't ignore what's wrong. These days I try to fix it the only way a person really can."

Redman sat down opposite him. "And how's that?" he said.

"In my self," McNamara answered. "In so far as I am able, I try to fix the wrong in my *self*."

Chapter Fifteen

5 November

As if in testament to the incendiary nature of events of the last two weeks, fireworks began to thunder and crackle over the University of Odium at 9pm. Watched by an awestruck gathering of upturned eighteen to twenty-one year-old faces, they boomed and blossomed over the University lake, like sketchy sparkling flowers filmed in time lapse against the darkened sky, each living and dying quickly in an ephemeral glistening gorgeousness, the report of each explosion quickening the heart and exciting the blood. The student body, insentient to the charms of political carousal to which the previous week had tempted it, did not remain immune to the alternative of gross physical arousal. Many of the minority of virginities which had somehow managed to remain intact for the first six weeks of term were finally lost that night. Ivy Littletot, who was no virgin, but was statistically much closer to virginity than she regarded right and proper, found herself in uncommon favour on account of her recent media exposure. Becoming increasingly drunk and convivial on tequila mixers, she enjoyed two straight offers and one queer flirtation, and before the night expired had rough sex with a male member of the SU

Executive. She did not know if it was the beginning of something that would last, but she was nonetheless grateful for the intrusion.

Sex was not on the mind of Jane Blake. The iron laws of supply and demand, inevitably advantaging girls like her over the Littletots of this world, meant that it seldom needed to be thought about. It could easily be found with the right look or word, and wallet. Ivy would have been bemused to know that Jane did not even want it, and had not really wanted it, in the sense of a genuine need or desire, for a very long time. What she wanted, on the contrary, was to escape its ravening clutches, to be no longer dependent upon it, to live in something closer to a state of chastity. She yet could feel stirrings of desire, but these were now for men who showed unusual restraint, who were moved, whether it be because of age or rectitude or fidelity or a certain elevation of being, only by things more profound and of greater lasting value. She had first felt it with McNamara, although with him it had seemed to take the form of unconquerable indifference towards her. Buckrack, however, she had clearly placed in a state of powerful emotion, albeit negative, filled with loathing for her, hate and cruelty. But these she could understand, in the circumstances. They did not diminish her growing respect for him, even while she suffered their effects. Now that he was safeguarding a course of action that would relieve her of those effects, and one that would provide a substantial sum of money for no sexual exchange of any kind, she began to feel a kind of new hope for a better life for herself. In a way, Buckrack might turn out to have been her redeemer.

As she sped south with him along the motorway towards Covet's second country retreat, Buckrack at the wheel of the hired car, she wished he was more amenable to conversation. She had hoped she might be able to make him understand her better, but he resisted being drawn by her gambit of trying to explain to him, in some kind of mitigation, why she had become what she had become. He was not contemptuous, however, rather purely purposive, focused on what had to be done. He curtailed her by saying that it was too late for such exculpations. She tried anew, telling him that she was intending to turn over a new leaf. He said it didn't matter to him. After that there was silence. They drove on, fireworks displays flashing up silently in the distant sky on left and right as they passed villages and towns on their route.

Buckrack became more vocal when he drew into a service station near the end of the journey, and bought them both coffee. What he spoke about was essentially practical, but she was glad to hear the sound of his voice. He was not any longer the seeming madman who had first kidnapped her and tormented her, dispossessing her of her identity, then monitoring her movements and actions and communications. Instead, he appeared keen simply to ensure that the meeting with Covet would conclude without any hitches. His warm American tones even reminded her of the homeland he had said he would be taking her on a plane to afterwards. She wondered as he talked if she would ever see him again there. She imagined he would not want that, but she felt an odd dissatisfaction that this and the flight might be the last time she would have any contact with his reassuring strength and confidence.

"He will want to talk to you," Buckrack was saying. "That's why he insisted on a last meeting. In a situation like this, the guy always wants closure. We'll let him do that. I will leave you alone with him, but I'll be listening right outside the door in case anything goes wrong. The thing you need to remember is not to deviate from the script we agreed."

"Yes," Jane said earnestly.

"He's almost certainly going to ask you why you submitted the Public Interest Disclosure when you did. He doesn't understand that. To his eyes it will seem a betrayal for which there was no motive and, looking at it objectively, it is. What's your answer to that?"

"I had a change of heart," she recited from memory. "I couldn't go on any longer, especially after what he wanted me to do with Dr Poon. I was in over my head."

"Right," Buckrack said. "But then he is going to ask why you didn't talk to him first."

"I meant to," she reeled off, "and in fact I tried. That's why I asked to see him earlier on the day I finally sent the document in. I was intending to explain. But it just turned into what it always turned into, lunchtime sex. I wasn't able to bring myself to tell him I wanted it all to end. Afterwards I felt degraded and demeaned, and I submitted the complaint in a state of despair."

"That's right," said Buckrack. "That'll do. He still won't understand it, but it will be enough. You weren't thinking straight, you were emotional and irrational, to the extent that you didn't even calculate too much the consequences for yourself. You don't give him any more information than that. If he wants to talk about other things you can say what you like: your past, your affair, his feelings. It's all very likely, but I know you've heard that sort of thing and dealt with it before."

"Okay." Jane felt herself blushing slightly. "But when it's done, when we leave, you will give me everything back, right?"

"Yes," Buckrack confirmed. He reached into his

pocket and handed her a slip of paper. "This is the changed password on your email account. Memorise it so that you can access it once you see him transfer the funds. You will then send an email to the Registrar withdrawing your Public Interest Disclosure: Covet will dictate the text. You can change the password to anything you want after that. Then we will drive off to the airport. The only reason I am getting on the plane with you is to make absolutely sure you leave as agreed. It departs at 6am. I have the tickets. I will give you your ticket and your passport at Heathrow."

"Can I see it?"

"The passport?"

"No, my ticket."

He looked at her disapprovingly, but put his hand into his inside pocket and brought out the tickets.

She looked at them both and said, "Did I have to pay for those? Did you buy them using my account?"

"No," he answered patiently. "I bought mine, and Covet paid for yours. I gave him your passport number and he had it sent to me."

"I see," she acknowledged. "Good."

He went on, "At the airport I will also give you the new password to your bank account. You can change the access codes again, so you will know you have sole control of the account before we are in the air. You can check at the same time that I have not touched your money, as I promised. I doubt if you'll be able to see the cleared funds for the international transaction by then, but you'll have witnessed him do it, and it's irreversible. You'll also get back your Facebook account – though you'll find that 'William Blake' is no longer in your list of friends, as he's deleted himself – and your cards and the rest. Once we clear customs at Boston, we'll part. And you'll never see me again. I have a return ticket."

Jane's heart sank slightly at this last piece of information, but she disguised it by expressing a more venal concern. "He will go through with it, right? He will transfer the money?"

Buckrack snorted gently. "It's taken him a week to make the necessary financial arrangements, but you'll get your fifty thousand dollars," he affirmed. "And so will I."

Covet had spent the last ten days viewing another three seasons of *Breaking Bad*. At first he had begun watching it when he was drunk, but he had had difficulty following the ins and outs of the plot, and twice he had fallen unconscious and woken up in the middle of the night with a nasty head to find the DVD looping its episodes mechanically, a situation he found degenerate, and which sharpened his sense of being out of control of things. He went back and started from season two again, watching in the afternoons, until he could stay away from the bottle no longer. Had he reached season five he would have felt some sympathy, as he paced his modest cottage, often talking to himself, flying into rages and unwitnessed outbursts, with Walter White stuck in the snow in a backwoods cabin in New Hampshire. As it was, however, in the lucid though depressed hours in which he had followed the narrative since, he found much to identify with in Walter's plight, especially his near continuous state of heightened anxiousness and paranoia. Walter's ability to get out of impossible spots by means of his own ingenuity and daring, overcoming his natural fears, impressed Covet mightily, were in fact a fillip which lifted his spirits each day before he downed more each night. The end of the last episode of season four, in particular, he found talismanic, as Walter, with cuts on his face and a plaster over his nose, told Skyler, in marvellous two-word sentences, "It's over. We're safe. I won." Covet vowed then not to watch the final season, if ever, until the current crisis was likewise over, he was safe, and he had won. The victory would come at a price, but at least he would not have to find a way to blow half of Jane Blake's body in two, the way Walter had Gus Fring's. And he would at last be able to get out of the horrible game he had been playing with himself and with others.

He heard the car door slam on the isolated road outside the cottage some time after eleven o'clock, and he waited tensely for the last few moments. The week had passed as such, like treacle pouring from a jar, as he made the mechanical, bureaucratic arrangements to gather enough money together, over sixty five thousand pounds in all, into an appropriate account from which he could pay Jane and Buckrack the fifty thousand dollars each that would be the cost of his reprieve. He was unused to waiting for anything, could normally demand things in double quick time. This, the final day, had dragged by in even slower motion. He had tried not to drink, but a quarter bottle of scotch had already passed his lips. Still, he did not feel too incapacitated, and took heart that it would soon be over.

He opened the door, which gave straight onto the living room, as he heard the crunch of their footsteps on the tree-sheltered gravel path. Jane stopped as she saw him framed in the light under the lintel, and stayed arrested a pace behind Buckrack, who turned and looked at her. He saw her eyes meet Covet's momentarily and then she bowed her head.

"It's okay," Buckrack said gently. "Let's go in."

Once inside, Buckrack indicated the armchair nearest the door. "Sit there," he told her. "And Sir Evan, I suggest you sit over there." Covet complied and took a seat several feet away. Buckrack remained standing.

The situation demanded a decent silence. Jane's knees were placed together and the palms of her hands were on them. Covet crossed his legs. At last he said, "Does anyone want a drink? I know I do."

"Not right now," said Buckrack. "There is a matter we need to deal with first."

He reached into his coat pocket and pulled out a small padded envelope. He upended the envelope, thus emptying its contents – a miniature video player, a memory card, and a small black circular bead mounted at the end of a one-inch pin – onto the coffee table which was between Jane and Covet.

"Sir Evan, you might remember that Jane asked to meet with you at noon in your usual hotel on the twenty-sixth of October."

Covet looked at him with an expression that said this was not a good start. "Did I tell you that?"

"You did, though you maybe don't remember. You were not, shall we say, in the best state of mind."

Covet relaxed. "Okay," he said.

"Do you know what this is?" Buckrack asked, pointing to the small black device on the pin.

Covet said, "No."

Buckrack looked at Jane and then back to Covet. "It's a wireless camera which sends a combined video and audio signal to this, the recorder. The files are high definition, much better than any cell phone could capture, and are stored on this memory card. You wear it like a brooch. It's hard to notice, especially on a woman's coat lapel, which is where Jane was wearing it when she knocked on your hotel room door that day."

Covet stared at him, then transferred his stare to Jane,

who was looking down at her hands.

"Yes," Buckrack said, "she was filming your tryst. She put her coat over a chair facing the bed."

Covet seemed about to gag. A vein on his temple was enlarging. He looked up at Buckrack again. "Have you seen it?"

"Some of it," said Buckrack. "Not all of it, but I had to check. It's clearly you and her. The duration is about ninety minutes."

Covet closed his eyes and sat forward, bowed, raising his right hand to his forehead.

"Don't worry," Buckrack continued. "The fact is, she told me about it voluntarily and gave it to me when I proposed the solution to your mutual predicament. She says she has not made any copies and I believe her. I did check her computer, her iPad and her phone, and there was no sign of a copy on any of them. Had she wished to hold onto it for any purpose she simply needn't have told me about it. Shocking as it is, I'd take it as a sign of her good faith."

Covet cried out incredulously, "*Her good* – ?"

Buckrack raised his hand. "Yes," he said. "However it may look, yes. But you have it now. I don't believe she does."

"It's true." Jane spoke softly for the first time. "I don't have a copy, and I'm very sorry."

Covet shook his head. "But *why* – ?"

"Sir Evan," Buckrack interrupted again, "perhaps you can discuss this in a few minutes. You simply needed to know about it first off. I don't think she would even use a copy if she had it. It hardly shows her in a good light either."

Covet relented. "Alright, but there are a few other things I need to get straight with her."

"Of course," said Buckrack. "We have some time if you two need to talk. But I think we should get the main business out of the way."

The pair sat silently with Buckrack standing over them. Neither moved. Covet continued to glare at Jane but she did not return the look.

"I understand," Buckrack cajoled, "that there is some justified bad feeling on one side, and some awkwardness on the other, but perhaps you two need to see this more as a simple business transaction. It's unpleasant, but these things happen. Sir Evan, you need to transfer the money to Jane's account. Then she will send the email."

Covet stirred himself resentfully and got out of the chair. "I've got it set up on the computer." He walked over to a desk on which sat a brightly lit laptop.

Jane did not get up but watched him from a distance. She was distracted by Buckrack gesturing with his hand for her to stand. "You need to see this," he said.

She walked with him over to the desk at which Covet was now seated. Both stood behind him.

"This is my current account balance," Covet said. "As you can see, it is over seventy thousand pounds. There is my name. This is your name, Jane, bank and account number."

Buckrack took Jane's bank card out of his wallet and handed it to her. She leaned over and checked the details against it.

"Okay," she said.

Buckrack held his hand out for the card and she returned it to him without question.

Covet continued, "You can see the sum to be transferred here – fifty thousand dollars. When I confirm the transaction you will see a message telling me that the transaction is final and that once I have confirmed again

209

the funds will be instantly withdrawn and cannot be returned. You will then see my new balance, which will be about thirty-one thousand five hundred pounds less – whatever the exact sterling equivalent of fifty thousand dollars is at today's exchange rate." He looked over his shoulder at her. "I am going to confirm the transaction now and I want you to check the text of the popup message."

Jane nodded. Covet moved the mouse and clicked once. Jane read the screen.

"So when I click one more time you should see the transaction go through and you can check the new balance," Covet resumed. "Then you will write that email I need you to write. Agreed?"

Jane assented once more. Covet turned, sighed, and clicked again. The three watched the transaction complete. Covet then surrendered the chair so that Jane could log onto her email account.

Once she had done so, he said, "Let's make it short and sweet. 'Dear Dr Asterisk, I hereby wish to withdraw the Public Interest Disclosure I submitted to you by email on 26 October. I was not in a balanced state of mind when I sent it, having not taken my prescribed medication for several days, which had placed me in a profoundly delusional condition. I wish to make it clear that the document is in its entirety dishonest and untrue. I am ashamed to have written it and would like to offer my humblest apologies both to you and anyone else who has read it and, most of all, to the Vice Chancellor for the acute offence and distress which it must have caused him. Yours sincerely.'"

Although he was puzzled by the wholly unhesitant and unquestioning manner in which Jane quickly typed and despatched the missive, Covet felt a certain small resurgence welling within, which began to displace his previous resignation. It was good to be dictating again. As she logged off, he turned away, and with something approaching actual breeziness said, "Perhaps we can have that drink now?"

Buckrack declined. "No, thank you. I'm driving. My work is also pretty much done here. I think I should give you two some time to talk alone and say goodbye. Jane, I will be just outside the door on the porch. I'll wait for you to come out, then we'll go."

He left. Covet poured Jane some scotch and sat opposite her again. Some of his lost *bonhomie* was returning, although it was tinged with sardonicism.

"I suppose you missed your regular pay cheque at the start of the month," he said. "But what I just did more than makes up for it, I imagine."

Jane eyed him coolly. She felt feistier now that the transaction was completed and Buckrack was on guard at the door. "What do you get paid, Evan? Seven hundred thousand dollars a year? It's not even a month's salary to you. It's what you would have given me had I stayed another two years."

"That's true," said Covet, "minus what I would have paid it for, of course." He sipped his drink. "I suppose I do have the video. Remind me, what did we get up to that day at the hotel?"

Jane's eyelids flickered. "It was one of your 'do as I say' days."

He smiled. "That should be quite a memento. But why?"

"Why what?"

"Why the video? Was it your plan to blackmail me all along?"

She answered, "No. But things went awry after Poon. I

wanted out. I didn't think you'd be agreeable. The video was meant to be for leverage rather than blackmail."

"I see," he said. "But then just a few hours later you submit a document to the University, recounting our history, but without the video? You go public? I don't get it."

She shrugged. "You might find it hard to believe, but I thought it was time for the truth. A man in your position? Doing the things you do?"

Covet guffawed in disgust. "A man in *my* position, Jane? What about your whole *Kama Sutra* of positions?"

"Yes," she said. "It's true. I have done very wrong things. But I don't hold much power over others, except for sex, which, believe me because I know, can only be used to control the already weak. I haven't ever deliberately set out to entrap men in ways I could use against them, to damage them in the eyes of others. I was selfish and uncaring, yes. I may have warped some of them, but not without their willing consent. What you were using me for was quite different. You made me a honeypot, a kind of snare. No one ever did that to me before. It's a step above the ordinary kind of lust. That's just bad, but you, well, you are wicked. I'm just a whore, no worse, no better."

He gazed at her. "And I thought..."

"You thought *what*?" she sneered. "Are you going to give me that old line? You thought I had feelings for you? Look in the mirror. Better still, look in your soul."

"No," he replied mutedly. "I was going to say something about my feelings. I thought I loved you."

She leaned forward in her seat. "You thought you *loved* me? First you pay me to fuck you, then you pay me not to fuck other people, then you actually *pay me to fuck other people*. Is that your idea of love? Giving me cash to seduce Krokoff? You didn't even stop at the humans with cocks. You loved me so much you wanted my tongue in Poon's hairy axe-wound as well. It wasn't love, Evan. I'm used to being treated like a sex doll, but to you I was a different kind of instrument altogether. Well, it's over, and if you expect me to sit here feeling sorry for you or eating humble pie, it's not happening."

His eyebrows raised an inch up his forehead.

"Look," she said. "You had your fun. I got my money. That's all it was ever about. It got a little complicated, but you've wriggled out of it. I learned what my limits are, and how I have to change. I'm not sure you have. I see no conscience in your eyes at all. You're like some kind of lizard or snake."

She got up. On instinct he arose as well and, ensuring that he left a gap between them over which they would not make physical contact, he crossed and opened the front door.

They both saw bright yellow, but Covet saw it better than Jane in the second they both had to take it in. Buckrack was standing ready in the porch, dressed from head to foot in oilskins zipped up to the neck, with a hood around his head. There was something in his gloved right hand, but neither had time to make it out properly before he lunged forward with the full weight of his body, emitting a loud empowering roar, throwing out his left arm to push Covet bodily over, and making one swift, decisive, upward movement from his waist with his right.

Jane's vision became cloudy at the edges. The surface of her body tingled with racing endorphins and her hearing instantly disappeared, or was rather obliterated by a kind of white noise. She looked and saw a thin black object slanting downwards to the right from the area between her navel and her chest. Covet, sprawling on the floor, saw it more as it was, the butt of a heavy kitchen knife buried up to the hilt. Jane looked up at Buckrack's face. He was removing the hood and staring at her with fascinated determination. His expression seemed to speak of a certain foreknowledge that had been denied her, although it also appeared, now that his features were blurring, to be forgiving her for something because her penance had finally been done. There seemed even to be a little regret or sympathy in his look. Her hearing returned slowly as the ringing in her ears faded. She was not aware of herself breathing. Her lungs seemed too full or too empty of air – she was not sure which – to make speech possible either way. She was making sounds of a sort, or rather her body, which now seemed a kind of foreign object, was producing involuntary noises from the throat, guttural, catarrhal. It took a step back. Neither Covet nor Buckrack moved. Her vision was narrowing even further, and her eyes opened wider in automatic compensation. Buckrack's eyes, conversely, seemed to narrow the more unblinkingly he watched her. There were now thick black rings encircling what Jane could still see, and what she could see seemed to be receding down a lengthening tunnel. Her body took another step back. Her hands dangled uselessly in front of her stomach, unable to make the journey all the way to the knife handle, and there was the first feeling of something hot and gushing, travelling down her belly beneath her shirt, then coursing around the waistband of her skirt, slightly ticklish. It seemed damp down there, but her neck was locked in position and she could not bend it to look. She became aware that her mouth had opened wide and she was unable to close it. Her jaw seemed paralysed and she thought she might be dribbling. She staggered back one more step, and her calf made contact with the edge of the coffee table. Her thighs felt weak and had begun to shake, so it seemed natural to try to lean back and sit on the table. As she did so, she found herself losing balance, wobbling and falling completely, her waist rolling across the wooden surface and momentum carrying the top half of her body further back, over the far edge, where her skull struck the arm of the easy chair with an upholstered thud and she lost consciousness, her head and shoulders on the rug, the rest of her body propped up over the table top. Her lower limbs had splayed as they gave way beneath her and left the floor, forcing open her coat, so that all Buckrack could see when she finally went inert was her bottom half, sticking over the far table edge, her skirt hitched up, her legs gaping wide at an obtuse angle, as they had too frequently been in life.

It was a very televisual death.

Chapter Sixteen

5 November

"What the *fuck* have you *done*?" Covet screeched.

Buckrack, still in his full oilskins, had been standing over the table, watching blood seeping along the torso of the upturned Jane, emerging from under her clothes, dark at the white skin of her exposed throat, flowing sideways into the reaches of her long brown hair. Now he looked over at Covet, his eyes narrowing once more, and pointed to the chair near the computer, the furthest from the front door.

"Sit down," he hissed, "and don't you move!"

Covet did as he was told and inched towards the seat.

Buckrack noticed that Covet was shaking. "Have another drink," he said, picking up the whisky bottle and pouring a large one, which he passed to him. Buckrack poured another and put it and the glass on the half of the table that was not occupied by Jane's jutting lower legs. He stepped out of the front door and brought in a small green denim shoulder bag, which he placed on the floor near the exit. He sat down and took a drink.

"This is the time for me to ask some questions," Buckrack said. "Then I'll fix this."

Covet sat doggedly quiet.

Buckrack asked, "Do you remember when we first met?"

Covet swallowed. His upper lip trembled. "On the plane from LA to London last summer. We sat next to one another in first class."

"And that was the first time you ever saw me?"

"Yes."

Buckrack first nodded and then shook his head. "It wasn't the first time I saw you." He reached into the shoulder bag and brought out two envelopes, one large, one small. "Have a look," he said, throwing the larger on the table.

Covet picked it up and pulled out a sheaf of white papers on which were printed various colour photographs showing him and Jane.

"That's you and her in Boston," he said. "Not the first time or the second time you met, but the third: you went there to start your second road trip together. Then there's one of you having lunch in Chicago. Drinks in Colorado Springs. It was wise to avoid some of the 66, all those cattle towns in North Texas, for example. But Silverton, where you stopped, see, for gas, is even better in winter, when the passes are snowbound. There you are kissing in Santa Fe, and holding hands in Flagstaff. Happy memories? You can keep them."

Covet, in agitation, mumbled, "But this was before you and I met."

"True," said Buckrack, "but I took them. You've read *Lolita*, right? You know, when Humbert takes Lolita off for a year-long road trip?"

"I, I, " Covet stuttered, "I think I saw the movie."

"Too bad," said Buckrack. "Neither version can compare, although I actually think the remake was far superior. Anyway, Humbert starts to understand, but too late, that someone was following them most of the time, another guy. That other guy was me, in your case."

Covet was visibly startled.

"I know," Buckrack assured him. "I've seen this so many times. You considered you were alone and, when you realise someone else was watching you, you start to think of what you did in more moral terms than you did at the time, or rather you always knew it was immoral, all the time, but you get frightened about the consequences of having been found out. It's a contrastive shock, because the immorality itself was so hedonistically satisfying."

Covet put the photos back on the table and his hands went to his face. He tried to compose himself. "Am I in some kind of trouble?" he asked.

"Are you," Buckrack repeated, "*in some kind of trouble*? There's a dead woman on your floor and her blood is ruining your carpet. Does it feel like you're in *some kind of trouble*?"

"I mean, a CIA guy was following me all across America. Why?"

"Ex-CIA," Buckrack reminded him. "Though technically, you're right. At the time I was still with the Agency. But I wasn't following you. I was tailing her. You never saw me, because I was always a fair way behind you. I simply put a tracker above the rear wheel of the car. While I was about it, I put a listening device under the dash. All those long drives, all those long conversations..."

Covet closed his eyes, then made an effort to open them again. "Why? Was she... was she some kind of *spy*?"

Buckrack laughed. "You've been watching too much television, Covet. She wasn't a spy."

"So... so you put her up to this? The two of you were in on it? To blackmail me?"

Buckrack scratched his head. "More and more. No, I am not the bigger conspiracy behind her smaller conspiracy with you. We were not a pair of happy-go-lucky con-artists, her and me. She didn't know me either then. Where do you get these crazy notions? Real life is less dramatic than that. She was a whore, who knew her market well. You were her client, or perhaps her victim. If that's the right word, I was simply another one of her victims. Let me show you something else."

He took a single photograph from the smaller envelope and held it out in his hand, displaying it to Covet across the table. This was a regular-size developed print, a family photo, all smiles, of a relatively young man and woman with a small baby.

"You can't have this one," Buckrack said. "Because that's my only son, his wife and daughter. He was an Assistant Professor at Amherst, in the Literature Department."

"*Was*?" said Covet.

"Yes. He shot himself in his garage last May. You're figuring it out, right?"

Covet's brow furrowed. "He...?"

"That's correct," said Buckrack, returning the photo to the envelope and then the envelope to the bag. "Happily married as he seemed to be, indeed as I think he was, it was not enough to stop him succumbing to her, what shall we call them, admissible attractions? Of course he wasn't rich like you. But he paid her in kind. He wrote her essays for her. Hence her magnificent degree. It all blew up in his face, of course. She cut it off with him almost as soon as she had the scroll in her hand. By that time she was fucking you and God knows who else. From the note he left – I was the one who found him, you see – his good feeling for his wife seemed entirely to have evaporated, he was, it seems, genuinely in agonising love with Penelope Pussylips here, or thought he was, but he was about to be found out, there was an investigation ongoing at Amherst, all causes for despair, and no one to talk to, the usual kind of suicide stuff. His wife doesn't know. It's better for her and my granddaughter that she doesn't. I kept the note to myself. It named our Cleopatra, though. I took it badly. The Agency gave me compassionate leave, but that only allowed me more time to think, perhaps not very well, perhaps morbidly, but then we're all human. You have two grown sons, Covet. You can imagine."

"I am sorry about your son," Covet said, as soberly as he could. "But revenge is – "

"They say many things about revenge," Buckrack interrupted. Then he jerked his thumb at Jane. "The dish on your floor is certainly getting colder by the minute."

Covet tried again. "Well, you've had your revenge, then, no?"

Buckrack pondered. "In a way. The problem with revenge, though, is that the revenger becomes engorged with a weird sense of justice. That's what revenge is, really: the pursuit of justice by irresponsible means. It gets conducted in a private, unaccountable manner, it becomes a law unto itself, a virtue that is at once a vice. You're a vengeful man yourself, Covet. McNamara – you wanted your revenge on him, for example. Then that impulse spread to others. You wanted your revenge on Poon, and to get that you put Krokoff, who as far as I know had done nothing you could personally feel even slighted by, in harm's way as well. Before you know it you start wanting the scalps of those who are even *associated* with the object of your revenge. I wonder where it leads if the revenger isn't stopped? Pehaps he even starts taking revenge on people *in advance* of any wrong they commit against him. Maybe I should better understand you by examining what's happened to myself."

Covet raised both hands defensively. "Look, you're not thinking straight. If you're talking about me, well, surely you've done enough to make me suffer? I think we've both been the victims here. I know what I did with her was wrong, and I've been almost ruined by it. You might not believe me, but I had come around to that understanding myself. Just before all this broke I had made a promise to myself not to go on with it, to try and make amends."

"Don't worry," said Buckrack. "I am not intending to prolong your suffering much beyond this conversation. But I do want to have it. It might help you comprehend things. As for you setting it all aright, what are we looking at here? In the last half hour what you've tried to do is extricate yourself. You haven't wanted to acknowledge the truth of what you did and live with the consequences of that truth. You've tried to cover it up so that you can continue. Oh, what, you're going to go on and build a new, more benign dispensation? On the basis of a massive falsehood? And what does that involve, more falsehood within falsehood? Getting rid of the dead body on your floor too, perhaps, so that it can't be connected with you? Suddenly, after a lifetime of slowly consuming corrosion, if you can get away with just one more deceit, the biggest of them all, you'll lead yourself by the hand into Damascus?"

Covet bit his lip. "I'd like the chance. Look, I was going to pay you fifty thousand. I'll double it."

"You'll pay me? You'll pay a man you think is called *Buckrack*? You still think that's my real name? Oh, what? You think an ex-Agency guy can't get a fake passport with any name he likes? The name I chose was even intended

221

as a provocation but, oh no, you respond to it like one of Pavlov's dogs. The bell of *Buckrack* sounds and you throw money at it. I have often wondered, in the time I have known you, how a guy who was once a distinguished Professor of Law became such a Lord of Misrule. But then I realised, not that you're stupid, but if anyone can get your attention and press the right buttons in you that you do act pretty stupid pretty predictably. Your vanity, that's the key, especially your failure to understand that power over people and controlling them are not the same thing. It makes you so easy to play. All that talk in the car with her I heard as I drove five miles behind you, you never twigged that she was the one in control, not you. She just knew how to do it. She had a gift for adjusting the narrative. You didn't notice how she suddenly changed the theme one day and started saying, even though she'd already blown your mind with her skilled sexual antics, that even greater things could happen if you were open to it? She was several moves ahead of you. You were going back to Nevada, the cocaine was already in the bag again, but the second whore she got for you that night, oh, that was a new high altogether. You know, the one that wasn't mentioned in the document she sent to Asterisk, the one whose head she held by the ponytail and pushed down on your cock while she fed you with her own tits? The one who obeyed every sexual command voiced to her by Jane, upon whom Jane encouraged you to visit the most extreme fantasies your mind could concoct? You think Jane didn't know that girl already, that the entire episode wasn't deliberately staged? It didn't cross your mind that the porno sandwich stunt was designed to break you, to unman you? You thought that was *real life*? And didn't the stratagem work, like the drugs had worked the previous year, when the entire crazy plan for you to bring her to England surfaced and was quickly consented to? As if that wasn't already a loss of judgment too many, didn't you now entertain delusions of potentially limitless power over others? Without stopping to think how Jane obviously knew that, unlike a wife, if you're going to stay with a whore, *it has to keep getting better*?"

Covet looked horrified. "How do you know about that night in Vegas?"

"You fool!" Buckrack spat. "You still don't know that she *told* me? You still think that *she* submitted the document to Asterisk, not *me* using her email account? It hasn't occurred to you that I *controlled* her? That I still control her bank account, for example, that you've already put fifty thousand dollars into, and which still has lots of the money you paid her this last year? That I know everything you did with her because I forced her to tell me? That the video camera she turned up to the hotel wearing in her lapel that day was given to her by me, and that her calling you to arrange the date was also her doing my bidding, while I recorded the whole liaison remotely? That she was acting under my instructions to make it as raunchy as possible?"

Covet glowered at him speechlessly. Buckrack got up and took the whisky bottle in his gloved hand. He poured two more measures and sat down again.

"You will appreciate," he went on, "how hard it was for me to keep my poker face that morning in Homestead Park when you denied virtually all knowledge of her, when I knew you had been playing sex games with her just the afternoon before. I'm not aware of the precise point at which I decided that you were probably worse than her. It's true that I was not in the best state of mind when I went to Boston to find her in the middle of June, after I used the resources available to me to discover she

223

was coming back to the States. I was grieving badly over my son's death, I was not sure exactly what I intended, but I pretty much stalked her in Boston while I weighed up the possibilities, and then, something which made everything immeasurably more interesting, in walked the man who turns out to be the Don Draper of Odium, not quite my inexperienced son, but someone who ought to have acquired more balance of mind and soundness of judgment, and who can definitely do a lot more harm to others because he hasn't. I knew all about you I could find within twenty-four hours. By the time the three of us had crossed the country together in our trans-American caravan I knew a whole lot more about you than I could ever find out from archived records and internet pages. I wasn't sitting in that seat beside yours on the flight to London by accident. You're so utterly naïve, Covet, such a soft touch. What did it take to hook you in as you sat there in the afterdaze of three and a half weeks of constant jizzum-squirting and strumpet-playing? A few hints about my history in the intelligence services, a business card for a fake consultancy referring you to an improvised website promising discreet solutions to corporate problems, one, just one follow-up call from me, a further single lunchtime meeting in London where I proposed that straightforward bugging of offices would probably end your Union troubles, and that all I needed to be able to do it for you was simple cover within your organisation? I flew back to the States and handed in my notice. I even took the three months' pay without being required to do a single further day's work: it ran out just last month. They were glad to let me go. I was nothing but grief-stricken dead weight by then, so the story went, and it was probably true. Eight weeks later I was a pseudonymous Professor in an English university fitted up with a research profile you and I jointly invented. And it got me real close to Jane Blake, with the added convenience that anything I might decide to do to her would not even be on my own soil or under my own name. There is no Cannon Buckrack in the USA. The real me is believed to be living in painful retirement back east. And when I step on that plane to Boston in the morning, I won't be using my return ticket, and Buckrack will cease to be, except for an English bank account into which the University of Odium will continue to pay salary for the next ten months, and which I will empty, as I will empty Jane Blake's. Not that I need the money. I intend to give that to my daughter-in-law. It'll be some compensation for her, but of the thinnest kind."

Buckrack's revelations, mingled with alcohol, had put Covet into a deep mental stupor. He felt like a barrier upon which wave after wave of guilt, then anger, then remorse, and finally fear kept crashing. He looked at Jane's stabbed body. "What are we going to do with her? Surely you can make her disappear too? I mean, you know how to do that, don't you?"

Buckrack smiled. "What I was going to do next depended on you. It would follow from your reaction when I told you all of this. I guess you need a few minutes to think about it. Have another drink while you do."

He stood up and refilled Covet's glass, recorked the bottle, and remained standing. Covet took a gulp. "I don't need time to think. I want you to get rid of the body. I'll help you if I have to. I just want her erased, along with the evidence. As I said, I will even give you more money, if that's what you want. I can handle things administratively after that, as long as she's not easily discoverable. No one knows she's here except you and me, right? Even if they find her, nothing more than circumstantial evidence will point to me. I know the law. And I didn't kill her, after all, whatever else I did. But I swear I won't mention you if I am ever asked."

"No one would believe you anyway," Buckrack said. "It would seem a tall story."

"That's true," said Covet. "So let's dump her somewhere."

Buckrack surveyed him one last time and said, "That's your solution? Are you sure?"

"Yes," said Covet. "She was trash anyway. No one will miss her."

Buckrack nodded.

With a movement which Covet did not have time to see, the two-thirds empty whisky bottle was transferred from one of Buckrack's hands to the other and brought crashing down on the top of his forehead with such force that it cracked open. Whisky spray stung into Covet's eyes, broken glass lashed his face and he slumped rightwards like a cow shot with a captive bolt pistol. He did not pass out entirely, but could only flail a little on the floor, quite impotent. He really did seem to see stars, as he remembered from childhood cartoons, and hear bells, or at least one prolonged drone that resounded un-ceasingly. He had a sense of Buckrack moving for his bag near the door. When he opened his eyes they seemed to be on fire, but he caught a glimpse of white cord, like TV aerial wire. He struggled to get up. Buckrack seemed a little way off, doing something with the wire, but Covet could not find his feet or even prop himself up on his arms. He then felt himself dragged bodily, Buckrack's gloved hands under his armpits, his oilskins rustling, and something tight being wound around his neck. The blood in his head seemed constricted, adding to the awful concussive pain, and his chest heaved for air. The old pain to the left of his solar plexus flared, hideously sharper than usual, as if something inside was about to burst open there. Buckrack was grunting loudly and straining. Covet felt himself seemingly hoisted upright by the force at his throat, suffocatingly, until he almost lost purchase on the surface beneath him, feeling it only with the balls of his slippered feet, his heels unable to reach it. The periodic wrenching at his throat stopped, and he felt suspended, his toes twitching as his feet tried to find something solid beneath them. A few moments seemed to pass. His pounding heart slowed a little and he was able to open his wet eyes. Buckrack was below him, looking up. Covet found himself perched in a standing position at full stretch on the coffee table, with what he guessed was the wire, acting as a noose, slung over one of the ceiling beams and secured he knew not how. He could see Jane's legs from the knees downwards sticking out stiffly to his left, but not the rest of her.

Between Covet's flickering eyelids, Buckrack appeared to be breathless and savage-faced with exertion. He bent down to the floor and took hold of one of the table legs, looking up as he did so. "I wanted you to be conscious at the end," he said. With that, he pulled the table leg hard towards him. Covet felt the slightest of jolts. Air popped in his cheeks as his throat contracted, then escaped as his lips flew open despite clenched teeth, and his head was flicked back. There was a brief rushing sound in his ears, like a recording being played in reverse, and he heard nothing else.

Buckrack got up from the floor and sat back in a chair to recover himself. He watched Covet spasm stiffly for a moment, then averted his eyes. Seeing that there was still some scotch in his glass, he swallowed it. Looking back, but only at Covet's feet, he saw that they were at last still.

He was sweating. He got up and went outside to find colder air. Some moments later he walked to the car, took Jane's suitcase out of the boot, and brought it in to the living room, laying it down in a corner. He unzipped it, took her passport, phone, keys, iPad and purse from his bag, and placed them in an inside compartment of the suitcase. Then he closed it again. He checked around the coffee table, taking the pinhead camera but leaving the other items. He picked up the empty glass he had been drinking from and put it in his bag. Satisfied, he stepped over to Jane and, bending down, gripped the handle of the knife and pulled. It came out surprisingly easily. He stood a while over the body, to let most of the blood from the blade drip on her rather than leave spots on the carpet. When it stopped he went to the back of Covet and, placing the handle against his dangling right hand, pressed the fingers and thumb in a fist around it. Then he let go and the knife fell to the floor.

He turned off all the lights and went outside again, leaving the door half ajar. A late fireworks party seemed to be in progress in the nearby village. He could hear the distant bangs and fizzes, but they were coming from the rear side of the cottage, so he could see only their peripheral illumination rather than the explosions themselves. In the open porch he pulled off his gloves and oilskins and put them in a refuse sack he took from the bag. He tied it and walked along the path beneath the trees. He reached the car, and put the bag and refuse sack in the boot.

Turning one last time to look at the house, he was just in time to see a single rocket shoot up into the sky above its roof, bursting in a glittering shock of white, purple and red, which was seen a few seconds before the deafening bang of its detonation reached him. Then there was the shrill metallic rustle as he watched its many sparks shower and fall and finally wink out, silver smoke spreading in their wake across the inky night sky. In the distance the spectating village crowd roared and clapped in approval. Their shouts and echoes too, eventually, died away. Just as the last of them did so, he heard a faraway tolling. The village church bell was chiming midnight.

EPILOGUE
8 NOVEMBER

Chapter Seventeen

8 November

It was a rare sunny November noontime, without cloud cover, and therefore cold. Standing on the corner by the O2 shop in Bigton High Street, Redman, holding a large envelope under his arm, scanned the pedestrians walking towards him from the direction of the University. Even if Asterisk came by car and parked, his final approach was most likely to be made on foot this way. At last he picked him out by his rather wombling gait, portly, padded further in a large brown winter overcoat. Asterisk was casting cautious glances from left to right in some trepidation, evidently, of being recognised. Redman toyed with the idea of doing the whole thing in public, right there in the High Street opposite a charity shop, partly to increase the Registrar's discomfiture, partly to minimise the time he had to spend in his company. But when Asterisk finally came up to him, and suggested they get out of the public eye pronto, he concurred pragmatically. They turned a corner and went into a cavernous coffee bar and found a seat in a corner behind an abutting wall.

"I don't see why we had to meet out here," Asterisk said. "A bit cloak and dagger, no?"

"Neutral territory," Redman offered by way of an explanation. "And after all, we know that some offices at the University tend to have listening devices in them.

What hasn't been cloak and dagger about the last few weeks?"

Asterisk tilted his head in sour recognition of an awkward truth. "You said on the phone that it was important, urgent even. I hope so. The place is in meltdown. This is my first day back and I can barely spare the time."

"It's not exactly Lehman Brothers," Redman countered. "But nonetheless I may be able to help you with our current fiasco."

"You?" said Asterisk. "How?"

Redman took some papers from the envelope and placed them on the table.

"These, I believe, are yours," he said. "Invoices addressed to you for three microdevices. These three microdevices, to be exact." He reached into his jacket pocket and showed Asterisk the small black receivers in a plastic wrapper in his open palm. "I have made copies of the invoices, but these are the originals. I'll keep the microphones unless you want to get legal about them." So saying, he returned them whence they came.

Asterisk had started a little, but now had put his thumbnail between his teeth while he slowly calculated what might be about to happen.

"How did you get these?" he asked, placing one index finger on the invoices.

Redman turned over the envelope so that its address side was face up. It read:

STRICTLY CONFIDENTIAL
Professor Robert McNamara
Warden
Coolwipe Hall
University of Odium
Odium
OD2 3PP

234

"Postmarked Odium, last Friday, first class," Redman added. "He picked it up when he went in on Saturday morning. But he found the prospect of talking to you too distasteful, so he passed the task to me."

"So McNamara knows?"

"Yes. He also agrees with us having the conversation we're going to have. I wouldn't be having it if he didn't. In fact, it was more his idea than mine, but I am persuaded."

"And Poon? She was the one who submitted the FOI about the bugs."

"No. She doesn't know we have the invoices."

"Why not?"

"She's an idiot."

"That's true, but she's an idiot who's on your side."

Redman sipped his latte. "I think the distinction between a union side and a management side is a bit behind the curve, in the present circumstances. The management side is virtually, and in one case literally, dead. You are the last man standing, as far as I can see."

Asterisk grimaced at the directness of the reference to Covet. "And now what? You want to use this to knock me over as well?"

"We could, of course. But what would that achieve? An argument could be made that we are now on the same side."

Asterisk tinkered with a spoon. "How so?"

"Well," Redman explained, "let's speculate on the outcome if we decide to make it public that we have the invoices. The first thing that would be established beyond any reasonable doubt is that you personally were responsible for Odiumgate. I know Covet was probably the one who ordered it, but his head has already rolled, as it were, and your Nuremberg defence is not likely to succeed. The lesser guilt of mere complicity would not save you. Even if it did, you would then have to explain why you suppressed the invoices in the face of a legally binding FOI request. That alone would make your position untenable. So I think the second inevitable consequence is that you'd certainly be out on your arse in a jiffy, and that last stroke in the clean sweep of existing management would leave the field entirely clear for Sir Norbert Conquest and the pecking hordes to ransack the carcass. The third thing that would come to pass is that Poon's Hero of the People status, which is looking a little shaky without the material proof, would be consolidated beyond measure, when in fact her lack of discretion and forethought is one of the things which has brought us to the current state of emergency we're in. It might occur to her members who will be made redundant by the raiding of the tomb that they would not have lost their jobs had she shut up, but that insight will probably come too late, and one thing is for sure, Poon won't be among their number. Getting rid of her would look like managerial vindictiveness. If Poon had these invoices for a moment, she'd do an instant Statue of Liberty pose with them right outside your office window. In short, if they are revealed, one more member of management goes down, but hundreds of staff jobs are lost, and the University's reputation is comprehensively destroyed. Why would I want that? I'm not being personally generous to you in offering to give them back to you. It's just that your head on a pike has very low value these days. Sorry to say that, but it's true."

"Alright," said Asterisk, "but how does giving them back to me solve anything?"

"It doesn't," Redman replied, "on its own. It gives you the choice, though. Let's say the invoices were, er, *lost*, and I'm simply returning them to their rightful owner. I don't intend to make it my business what you choose to do with them. You might let your dog accidentally chew them, for example."

"Why don't *you* just destroy them?"

"No," Redman said brusquely. "I mentioned that to McNamara, but he insists that his hands must be clean, and I agree with him."

"But if I don't give them up I'm in default of FOI."

"Which is no different from where you are right now, without your pretence to yourself that the papers mysteriously disappeared. We both know that you agreed with Buckrack that he would remove them."

Asterisk said, "You *know* about Buckrack?"

"I know," Redman said, "that it's his handwriting on the envelope. Quite why he should remove them, seemingly for your benefit, and then hand them to us, patently not to your advantage, remains a question I was hoping you might answer. Did you guys fall out over something?"

Asterisk was wide-eyed. "It's complicated. It's best to leave Buckrack out of all this."

Redman considered. "Okay," he said, "to be continued."

Asterisk pulled the papers a bit closer and looked at them cursorily. "What you are saying is that you are giving me these documents back and yet you still want me to do nothing with them? So why have you kept copies? If I don't divulge them you could simply produce your copies later to expose the fact that they were suppressed by me."

"I could do that *now* with the originals," said Redman. "The copies are just a form of insurance."

"You mean for future twisting of my arm, that's it, isn't it?"

"No," Redman said. "Just personal insurance for me and McNamara. You won't be dealing with me in future. After this meeting I'll be resigning my membership of the Union. Recent events tell me that it's not something I want to be involved with any longer. This is the last act I'll perform in an official Union capacity. But I want to make it clear. All I'm doing is giving you the papers back. I am not telling you exactly what to do with them. I just hope you'll act swiftly on a choice to do the right thing with them, which is nothing."

"Which is to do the *wrong* thing?"

"But for the right reasons this time. And to do it quickly. If Poon's FOI request can be responded to soon, like today or tomorrow, and you confidently declare no knowledge of any bugs or any record of their purchase, then it will settle much of the present disorder. Poon will be out on a limb. The staff will come back to work. Baum's death has been eclipsed by Covet's, and the manner of his could be presented so that he seemed the one bad management apple. You can blame anything negative on him: dead men tell no tales. You can get the University lawyers on Conquest's case and force him to back off, even go for a judicial review of the Department for Education's decision to appoint him Acting Vice Chancellor. If you start fighting now it may limit the damage, and we probably won't lose too many students."

Asterisk stroked his jaw. "And what assurance do I have that you're not just setting me up for a fall later? I do what I can to fix all this now, then when we've recovered ground in a few months, you spill to the press about my true role?"

Redman sighed. "I guess you have to trust me when I say we won't. We really don't care that much anymore, McNamara and me, and we won't be talking to Poon. So trust us if you can. If you can't, so be it. But there is an opportunity to stop the rot. I think you should take it. You can, on the other hand, play straight and release the documents, but that would simply end your career in ignominy right now. So what have you to lose?"

After a time Asterisk nodded slowly, and prepared to leave. But Redman put his hand on his elbow. "Not yet," he said. "There was something else."

Asterisk remained at rest.

"It's about Covet," Redman continued. "Perhaps just to satisfy my curiosity, if nothing else. There was the weekend TV news, of course, and this morning's papers. But they were very thin on details. Nothing much other than the postman finding him hanging in his cottage with Jane Blake stabbed to death on the floor. What more can you tell me?"

Asterisk was initially hesitant. "It's a bit hush hush, as you can imagine. The police called me yesterday. That's why I'm in today. We had a Management Board meeting this morning. I say that, though it was only me and Conquest, really. But, hell, we are going public with everything later this afternoon, so it hardly matters anymore, the details will be in the public domain soon. I suppose Buckrack told you about the PID?"

"No," Redman said. "He didn't."

"No?" said Asterisk. "For the life of me, I can't work that man out. He's very unpredictable. I'm banking on him keeping his mouth shut. If I can I'm going to give him a very wide berth in future."

"The PID?" Redman prompted.

"The PID was from Jane Blake," Asterisk said. "She and Covet had been having some sordid affair for over a year. The police already had it down from the crime scene as a straightforward murder plus suicide, and the PID pretty much supplied all the motive they needed on his part. They were not as flummoxed as I was by the fact that she withdrew her allegations by email on the same night they both died, because apparently he had just paid a whopping sum out of his bank account into hers before she did that. So it seemed to have got to the blackmailing stage. Something must have turned bad after that, on the night itself. They were drinking. It looks like she attacked him with a bottle and he stabbed her, or, well, it's hard to imagine he stabbed her then she managed to hit him with a bottle, but I suppose it could have been simultaneous, or she reached for the bottle when he threatened – doh, what's the difference? It hardly matters. Then he hanged himself. There were pictures of them together at the scene which corroborate the PID, even a video of them having sex, apparently. The blackmail materials, I imagine. It'll be in all the papers tomorrow once we release the full text. I have a press conference in the morning."

Redman thanked him for the information. "Did you know she told McNamara she was having an affair with Poon?"

"That's in the PID," Asterisk said. "Though apparently it wasn't true. The girl couldn't bring herself to sleep with the stupid bint. It's all very complicated. But rest assured Poon doesn't come out of it well. McNamara does, though."

Asterisk was opening his briefcase to put the invoices inside. "In fact," he said, fishing a document out, "why not read it for yourself? You'll soon be able to anyway. Here it is."

He handed the Public Interest Disclosure document over the table and picked up the invoices. Redman glanced through the pages but was interrupted by

Asterisk asking, "Buckrack didn't send you an invoice for a camera and recording equipment?"

"No," said Redman.

"You don't know anything about that?"

Redman shook his head.

"Oh," said Asterisk. "Good! One less thing to worry over."

He was about to leave, but turned around before doing so, and said, "You know, Covet was an awful man. I can't say I'm sorry he's gone, even spectacularly gone. A terrible bully. A total shit. It's not nice to say, but I can't imagine there's anyone who loved him. I'm convinced even his family didn't. He made me do lots of things I'm not proud of. You're aware of the kind of stuff I mean. I wanted you to know that it often wasn't the real me you were often faced with. In the universities I was taught in and worked in before these things couldn't have happened. With him off the scene, I think I have a chance to do things right, to help run the place with a renewed sense of decency."

Redman looked at him with the most finely calibrated expression Asterisk had ever seen: the face registered twenty per cent approval, twenty-nine per cent scepticism, and fifty-one per cent dubiety.

"You can try," was the reply.

"The novel that simply cries out to be a TV mini-series ... the *House of Cards* of the modern British university ... a thrilling satirical exposure of the witless evils of today's academy."

TV FOR TOMORROW

"Clockman has done it again! It's all here: the obloquy which taints all who choose to serve in today's university; the tyranny of social media; Brexit; the banal realities of modern anti-terrorism; even a zombie and ripe evidence that the #MeToo movement is an understatement. I laughed all the way through then wrote my resignation letter."

T(R)OPICAL LITERATURE

"At last Clockman's great comic trilogy is concluded. Quentin Tarantino meets the campus novel in an ecstatic renovation of the genre. Gone is all the humanistic twaddle and intellectual imposture which have beset the depiction of universities in fiction since day one. In their place we get the modern institution in all its cold-blooded malice, mean-spirited calculation, narrow-minded prejudice and, ultimately, maniacal self-destructiveness."

PSYCHOTEXTE

Now available in one volume as *The Odium Trilogy*

Made in the USA
Monee, IL
23 June 2025